CHRIS IN CANADA

CHRIS IN CANADA

BY

GEORGE FREDERICK CLARKE

ILLUSTRATED BY

EDWIN TAPPAN ADNEY

EDITED BY

MARY BERNARD

CHAPEL STREET EDITIONS

Published by
Chapel Street Editions
150 Chapel Street
Woodstock, NB E7M 1H4

www.chapelstreeteditions.com
chapelstreeteditions@gmail.com

Library and Archives Canada Cataloguing in Publication

Title: Chris in Canada / by George Frederick Clarke ; illustrated by Edwin Tapan Adney ; edited by Mary Bernard.

Names: Clarke, George Frederick, author. | Adney, Tappan, 1868-1950, illustrator. | Bernard, Mary, 1941- editor.

Description: Originally published: London: Blackie & Son, 1925. | Includes bibliographical references.

Identifiers: Canadiana 20210235233 | ISBN 9781988299358 (softcover)

Classification: LCC PS8505.L39 C45 2021 | DDC jC813/.52—dc23

Cover illustration by Edwin Tappan Adney

The text is set in Adobe Caslon.

Book design by Brendan Helmuth

To

My Mother and Father

Editor's Dedication

To My Lifelong Friends
Michael Clark, Pat Clark Samson,
Shirley Clark and Marc Samson

*Pat and Michael are my oldest friends—I've known
Michael since we were both two, and Pat, who is
two years younger, since she was a toddler. We played
together every summer when we were children, and
we've kept in touch ever since. My friendship with
Shirley and Marc is almost as long-standing;
I've known them since Michael married Shirley
and Pat married Marc .*

Contents

Editor's Preface

My grandfather, George Frederick Clarke (GFC), wrote *Chris in Canada* almost a century ago. It was his first book to be accepted for publication. He had been writing and publishing short stories in magazines for some time, but this book marks the beginning of his real success as a writer. The story follows eight months in the life of a boy of fourteen who has just immigrated, with his family, to a New Brunswick farm on the edge of a vast wilderness of woods, lakes and streams. He is eager to learn Canadian farming ways—and to go adventuring in that wilderness. GFC was writing about people, places and a way of life he knew well. *Chris in Canada* became one of his most successful novels.

In preparing the book for republication, I have worked from the first edition, silently correcting a few typos. This new edition has an Editor's Afterword with information about the book's background and the cultural context in which it was created. Keith Helmuth has contributed a Publisher's Afterword reflecting on the book's contribution to a distinctively Canadian, and New Brunswick, literature of place.

About the words "Indians" and "Melicete"

In recent times the Indigenous People of the St. John River region of New Brunswick have re-established "Wolastokwiyik" as their traditionally correct name, and "Wolastuk" as the correct traditional name for the river that Champlain named the St. John. However, George Frederick Clarke lived before the terms First Nation and Indigenous People were in common use. He called First Nation people Indians, and it was what they then called themselves. I have not changed his usage. During his lifetime the Wolastokwiyik were called Maliseet. (GFC spelt it "Melicete" in his writing of the 1920s and "Maliseet" thereafter.) Again, I have not changed his usage.

"Wolastokwiyik" is pronounced approximately as "Wool-AHS-to-gwi-ik," and "Wolastuk" as "Wool-AHS-took."

About Noel Polchies's dialect

Noel Polchis is a leading character in this book. He was a real person, a chief of the Wolastokwiyik below Woodstock. He was born about 1860 and died in 1927, a year after *Chris in Canada* was first published. He did not learn English till he was an adult, and used it only to transact business with White people or when talking with White friends, like GFC. In this book he speaks the non-standard English he spoke in life, transcribed by GFC in a spirit of love and respect. I discuss the issue further in my Afterword.

Footnotes and Endnotes

I have added informative notes in the text, at the foot of the page. They are marked with numbers. Notes marked with letters (a, b, c, etc.) will be found at the end of the book. They refer to sources, or to the geographical coordinates of places. (I have credited Wikipedia by name at the ends of footnotes rather than adding URLs, and the Oxford English Dictionary simply as OED.)

I have also included a Geographic Addendum about the correct names of three hills mentioned in the book.

Mary Bernard
February 2021

ILLUSTRATIONS

Cover   "The Moose Call" by Edwin Tappan Adney, oil on canvas, 1893, photographed by Mary Bernard, 2007

Maps   Annotated by Mary Bernard. Adapted by Brendan Helmuth. Source: Natural Resources Canada, Canadian Center Mapping and Earth Observation group.

Chapter 1

A Welcome

The high farm wagon, drawn by a pair of heavy draught horses, was slowly climbing what the loquacious driver had informed Bob, who was seated beside him, was the last hill on Howland ridge.

"Leastwise," he added, "that's the last civilised hill. Of course the road goes on. But it ain't a highway[1] after it enters the woods. It's called a portage" (he pronounced it portash) "and goes right through to the Nashwaak and the Miramichi. Nothin' but woods and lakes. Good huntin' country. Got a moose over at the Branch two falls ago—"

Chris, seated on one of the crates behind them, heard the man, who had been introduced to them as Bill Cummins, tell how he'd "called" the bull out just at daybreak and "fixed" him with one shot, right through the heart, that he had a spread of forty-seven inches, pans as broad as a tea-tray, with eighteen points. "Yes, sir, a record moose for these parts."

The boy was gloriously interested as well as puzzled. He had no reason to doubt Bill Cummins' veracity, and yet, how could Bill "call" a moose? Moose belonged to the elk family, and, of course, must be wild. Was it possible Bill was having a joke at their expense? But Bill Cummins was continuing in a dry, matter-of-fact voice.

---

1   The Howland Ridge road was, and still is, a gravel road. In this century "highway" usually means a paved major road between towns, but in the early twentieth century it meant any public road. GFC uses it in this sense throughout *Chris in Canada*.

"And deer? Lashin's of 'em. Got a ten-point buck last fall down by Taffa Lake, just as he come out for a drink; hit him through the lungs and he went—"

Where the deer went, what his ultimate fate, Chris didn't hear just then. His eyes were roving over a broad expanse of forest, miles and miles of it; over a succession of tree-covered ridges that rose here and there to lofty peaks. The kaleidoscopic view he had had of the forest through the train window had conveyed to him nothing of the immensity at which he was now gazing. Straight ahead—on his right as well as on his left—as far as his eyes could see, there was nothing but forest; a mute mysterious wilderness that set his pulses throbbing and his brain to conjuring within those silent fastnesses all the animals of which he had ever heard or read.

"By Jove! Stop!" It was Bob who had spoken. Bill Cummins applied the brakes and brought the horses to a standstill on the very crest of the hill. He turned inquiring eyes on Bob.

"What?" he questioned.

Bob was exclaiming over and over: "What a view! It's magnificent—magnificent!"

Bill merely grunted, "Quite a little nest of hills, eh?"

Bob turned to Chris with, "We'll have some jolly larks in those woods, kid," and to Bill, "Is that the lake down there?"

It was Taffa Lake,[a] replied the informing Bill, where he'd hit the ten-point buck through the lungs and had to follow him over the opposite ridge, and down into a swamp before he got him.

Chris had withdrawn his eyes from the forest, and was taking in the immediate scenery before them—the brown fields stretching down to the ice-bound lake, a dilapidated farm-house and out-buildings. As he thought, "Can it be possible that human beings live there?" a thin column of smoke suddenly shot from the stove pipe drunkenly protruding through the roof.

Bill Cummins said: "They've got a fire goin' already."

"They?" Whom could he mean? Not—surely not his parents—? And then, as to his unspoken question, Bill said: "Yes, that's your place," and, releasing the brakes, told his horse to "Giddap."

Chris's heart was like lead. That desolate-looking house the home for which they had exchanged the cheery, whitewashed cottage in Lincolnshire! There must be some mistake. Bill Cummins was only spoofing them. The lad's eyes skipped across the highway. In the little valley on his right were two houses much neater in appearance than the first, with chimneys of brick, but not at all like the pretty cottage back home. A half-mile away, on the height of land in the last clearing on the ridge, was another weather-stained house, dreary-looking enough. Surely not that either!

Was this the land of opportunity to which Bob had begged his parents to come? Was this the land, a part of the Canada, which, according to Bob, stood with eager arms outstretched to the Motherland for more settlers to till her soil? Brood of the Anglo-Saxon were wanted, so that the country should retain those liberties dear to the British heart. Oh yes, he had been thrilled, had felt himself a pioneer, a trail blazer, one who was to help—in his little way—to lay more firmly the foundation of Empire begun when Wolfe died on the Heights of Quebec.

Now he was conscious of Bob's voice: "The agent told us it wasn't much of a house; but I didn't imagine it was quite so—so run down. Of course, we'll have to build another right away."

"Yeah," ejaculated Bill Cummins. "But it ain't so bad. Nobody livin' in it since White left three years ago. But the land's good. Oh yes, first-rate land. Only needs workin' and fertiliser. Let's see." He swung round on Bob, a droll look in his pale-blue eyes. "You ain't just city Johnnies—you farmed some, didn't you?"

"Oh yes," answered Bob, "we had a farm under lease back home."

Bill spat dexterously into the ditch flanking the highway, hum-hawed a moment, then said: "Trouble with so many of you English folks comin' here, you think because you farmed in England, you can't learn anything more." He paused, adding oracularly: "When a chap thinks he knows it all, he don't know nothin'." He paused again, took out a plug of tobacco, bit off a big piece with his strong teeth and went on in a confiding voice—a voice that robbed his words of some of their sting: "You see, conditions is different here. What with early an' late frosts, a man's got to take a bit of advice at first. A lot of you chaps comes over and begins specialisin', starts raisin' cattle or sheep or hay, potatoes or grain. That's where you make a mistake. This country—I mean this Province of New Brunswick—is best for mixed farmin', hay an' oats an' potatoes an' buckwheat."

Though Chris's eyes were fixed wonderingly on the forest, he was taking in every word that Bill Cummins uttered. Bill was telling of an English family who had taken a farm out Maplewood way. "Guess they thought summer was goin' to last all year," said Bill. "They'd git up at eight in the mornin', start ploughin' or harrowin' bout nine o'clock, then knock off in the arternoon, 'bout four, for a cup of tea. Had one man to drive the 'osses, an' another to lead 'em by the head." Bill gave a snort of disgust. "I tried to tell 'em they'd have to work early an' late, and how the man that was engaged leadin' the 'osses could be doin' something else. Wouldn't listen. Grandfathers had done it that way, so they wasn't goin' to change. 'Course they couldn't make a go of things, an'—Gee there, Bess; Gee, Harry."

He guided his horses over a wooden culvert bridging the ditch, turned in between a couple of sad-looking gate posts, and sent them at a gallop down a muddy lane towards the house which Chris had fondly hoped might not be their new home.

He could now see the two-seated buckboard in which his father and mother, in company with the agent, had preceded them over the ridge. The thought of his mother—she who had always joyed in having things neat and clean—coming to this half-ruined habitation, made him heart-sick, cancelled the joy he had felt in gazing at those miles of forest. Then the horses came to a stop. He clambered miserably to earth, dragging his bag with him, flung it over his shoulder and walked towards the house.

He was yet a few feet away when his mother framed herself in the doorway, and, wonder of wonders, she was smiling!

"Welcome home, Chris," she said gaily. Then her eyes fastened on his face. With a bound he was at her side. She put her hand on his shoulder, gave it a gentle pressure, and with a quick glance at Bob, descending to the ground by way of the wheel hub, whispered: "We mustn't let *him* see we're disappointed; not the least bit, Chris lad."

The boy, gazing awesomely[2] into her serene countenance, said: "Mother, you're a brick—a regular brick!"

---

2   Awesomely means "in a manner which inspires awe" [OED], but GFC regularly uses it to mean "awe-struck" or "in awe".

CHAPTER 2
CHRIS SETTLES DOWN

The sun had long since gone down. Seated in the small kitchen about the stove (which was crackling merrily) the immigrants talked and watched the twilight hour giving way to dark. Chris, seated on a packing-case, hands clasped about one up-drawn knee, was gazing, tired-eyed, over the grey landscape to the forested ridges across the lake, that, according to Mr. Cummins, ran unbroken for a hundred miles. And here they were—he and his parents and Bob—set down on the very edge of it all; only one other farm between them and the wilderness. Millville, where they had got off the train, was but a village; the nearest town was twenty-five miles away. And Millville, though only three miles distant, might be a thousand miles for all one could see of it, so shut in were they by the hills. A feeling that had possessed him earlier in the evening, as of one standing on the verge of great adventures, again gave place to one of intense loneliness. Were there other boys his own age on the ridge? If there were, would they accept him, be chums with him? Or would they, like that girl at the station, regard him as an outsider?

Never, he told himself, would he forget that girl. (She must be only a year or two younger than himself, perhaps twelve years old.) In fancy he could see the drab little station; the crowd of curious onlookers grouped about their crated household things, which the train men were unloading; the bobbed-haired girl's pretty face upturned to that of her older companion; and her voice, he could hear it now:

"English Johnnies. Immigrants. See his new leggin's, Miss Allen, I wonder if he says 'Yes, by Jove!'"

He withdrew his eyes from the forest, let them rest a moment on the lake, then turned, glanced at his mother, enjoying, for the first time in her life, the sensation of sitting in a rocking-chair—a rickety thing left by the late owners of the house. She seemed quite happy and contented as she rocked back and forth in quiet-voiced conversation with Bob and his father. He noted the tired lines about her eyes, the wrinkled hands clasped in her lap. She must be quite done up and ready for a night's sleep. But, oh, she was courageous! He remembered her words standing in the doorway that morning: "Welcome home," and her whispered entreaty to him not to let Bob see that they were disappointed with their new home. "Yes, she is a brick," he repeated to himself. And whatever life in this place held for him, he must keep a stiff upper lip and play the game.

Half an hour later he went up the shaky stairs to the bedroom that was to be his.

He slept, after a while, and dreamed that he was once more in the train, which this time was bumping its way over the uneven road-bed towards St. John and the boat that was to take him back to England. And he wasn't at all happy. He felt that he was a deserter from a great plan in which he had been assigned an important part. England? Yes, he loved it, wholeheartedly; but he was a soldier, a link in the great chain of Empire development, and he must get away from his captors—somehow (oh yes, he was a captive) and go back to the farm on the ridge. There was ploughing and seeding to be done and there were those ridges across the lake to be explored.

Chapter 3

Noel Polchis

They were seated about one of the unopened boxes in the small kitchen the following morning, finishing breakfast, when, with a preliminary tap on the door, a man entered—a short, broad-shouldered man with bright blue eyes sparkling in a face tanned as brown as a nut. He nodded, removed his broad felt hat, promptly sat down, took out a briar pipe, a plug of tobacco and a knife, and, as he whittled the brown shavings into his palm, said:

"I just run over to say how-do, and get acquainted, and see if there's anything I can do to help you get settled. I live across the way. Clowes is my name—" He paused, shifted his knife to the left hand, holding the tobacco, rose and solemnly shook hands with Mr. Alison, Mrs. Alison, Bob, and Chris; then he again seated himself near the door, and, as he rolled the weed in his brown palms, went on:

"Sort of strangers in a strange land, eh? Must a been pretty tough breakin' up the home ties. But you come to a fine country. This ridge ain't like it was when I come here—" He forced the tobacco into the bowl of his pipe with a stubby forefinger, lighted a match, and, while the smoke wreathed his kindly face in a fragrant blue, continued:

"Nothin' but wilderness when my father come here fifty year ago. Had to chop down the trees to make room for a house.[3] Log house with a hole in the roof to let the smoke through. Later, we got a stove. That road—" he pointed through the

---

3   Like GFC's Loyalist great-grandfathers.

window to the highway—"wasn't there. Only a trail used by the Indians and trappers to get to the lakes and streams farther on." He paused, nodded to Mr. Alison, asked for a match to light his pipe, which had gone out, and went on:

"I remember—I was only four years old at the time—my father carried me over the ridge in his arms. That summer we had about half an acre of buckwheat growin' between the stumps of the trees he'd cut down. And at night we could hear the wild cats howlin' outside. Once a bear come in the early mornin' and killed the only cow we had. I remember Mother cryin'. And the next night Father got his muzzle-loading gun, went out and waited for the bear to come back. He did; just about midnight. There was a full moon and Father could see him plain. He shot him through the head."

Mr. Clowes paused again, smiled at Chris's intent countenance and added: "We used his skin for a bed coverin' many a winter night." He ceased, to light his pipe again, took a few whiffs, and said to Mr. Alison and Bob:

"Well, you got a pretty good farm; quite a piece of timber at the lower end of the lake. Must be quarter of a million feet of good spruce logs." He touched lightly on the lumber market, said that though the price of merchantable lumber was less than that prevailing during the War, it was yet very good; and, rising, said he must "be goin'." If there was anything he could do to help out the newcomers, all they had to do was mention it; added that he hoped they'd find him a good neighbour, and, as he bade good-bye to Mrs. Alison, said he'd send his Missus over to call.

"We'll try not to let you get lonely. We have the school teacher, Miss Allen, boardin' at our house. Winnie, that's our girl, not to mention half the young men on the ridge and in Millville, is head over heels in love with her."

Again, as when he had heard the bobbed-haired girl call them "English Johnnies" and refer to Bob's leggings, did Chris feel his face grow hot and uncomfortable. So her name was Winnie, and her home was on the ridge just across the highway! Pretty? Oh yes; but cheeky and ill-bred. He heard his mother inform Mr. Clowes that she already had met Miss Allen, saw Mr. Clowes clap his slouch hat[4] on his head and, followed by Bob and his father, go out. Then the boy rose, picked up his cap, opened a small door on the lake side of the house, and stepped out.

A path led over the soggy, brown field in the direction of the frozen lake, which, this morning, he could see was fast melting under the hot sun. His eyes roved over its surface, followed its inlet, that ran a half-mile or more, a narrow ribbon of blue, between a low-lying barren, with here and there dead trees rearing grotesque branches skyward, and stunted spruce and other evergreens which to him were then nameless. Half-way up the inlet, he could see a yet smaller ice-bound stream that wound snake-like north-westward over the barren, ultimately to disappear in a green growth of soft wood that formed the vanguard of a succession of tree-sentinelled ridges, that went on and on as far as his eyes could see.

Suddenly, directly over his head, he heard a whir of wings, a weird honk-honk! He gazed upward; a V-shaped flock of big birds, their long necks outstretched, their wings beating in perfect unison, were headed straight across the lake.

Honk!—honk!—honk!—honk! It was the homing cry of the Canadian goose, bound farther northward from the rice swamps of the south.

The boy watched them, a little nameless thrill pulsing through his body. Over the lake he saw the leader drop back, the one behind take its place. He saw them clear the opposite

---

4   A broad-brimmed hat with one side pinned up to the side of the crown.

ridge, soar above a mountainous peak, and gradually become a series of mere specks which at length vanished utterly in the blue.

Slowly the lad walked down the path, came to one of those odd-looking fences of split cedar logs zigzagging across the field, clambered over it, found the path on the opposite side and followed it until, a few hundred yards from the lake, he reached a small wood. He stopped, his ear bent to catch a distant tinkle and murmur, that sounded like a brook, on his right.

He left the path, entered the woods—maple and birch and ash and alders, with a sprinkling of young spruce and fir—steering his course towards that lilt of running water. The ground sloped gradually, and presently he glimpsed it through the trees—a mocking, laughing brook that tumbled, a series of miniature waterfalls, and wound a wayward course between tree trunks and boulders, down a little valley that ran diagonally towards the upper part of the lake.

The boy followed its downward course, came to a tangle of alders, forced his way through, stopped, startled, as something from almost beneath his feet went hurtling through the bushes. Just a glimpse he got of the bird; but it was enough. With a muttered: "That partridge gave me a jolly bad scare!" he began searching about for the nest. For he knew enough about game birds to know that this was the hatching season. Sure enough, behind a fallen log, in a bed of old leaves and small dried branches, he saw the eggs—ten, white as snow. He picked one up, put it against his cheek, muttered: "How jolly. There'll be partridge shooting in September," replaced the egg, and, with a smile on his lips, sought the brook again.

Suddenly he smelled smoke—the acrid stench of burning pitch, and presently, in a little clearing almost on the very apex of the point,[5,b] he saw a man bending over a fire. Something long, boat-shaped, lay, bottom up, on the ground. As he watched, curiously, he saw the man rise, holding in one hand a stick, one end of which was passed through the handle of a small black kettle. The man walked over to the boat—Chris was now sure it was a boat of some sort—and setting down his kettle, picked up what looked like an iron poker, dipped it into the kettle and began to daub some thick-looking mixture on the bottom of the frail-looking craft.

Chris approached. The man looked up. He showed no surprise at the lad's coming, merely said in a low voice: "How do?" and bent again to his task.

From pictures of Indians which Chris had seen in papers and magazines at home, he knew he was face to face with one of the natives of the soil. There was no mistaking those high cheek-bones, that straight nose, and the coarse black hair showing beneath the soft felt hat. And yet, where were the feathers, the buck-skin shirt and trousers, the tomahawk and scalping knife? This Indian's garb was like that of any labourer, save that on his feet he wore heelless moccasins. Oh, well, it didn't matter. The fact that the Indians no longer wore the romantic costume depicted in some of the stories the boy had read, meant only the destruction of one more illusion.

He said: "Good-day," in response to the man's brief salutation, stood watching him running the sticky, smelly substance along the seams of what he now realised must be a bark canoe.

It was all quite wonderful. He glanced about him and saw, stretched on a pole between a couple of saplings, a weather-stained piece of tarpaulin in the form of a tent or lean-to. On the ground beneath was a bed of green boughs over which were spread a couple of blankets. To one side lay a few blackened

---

5   The point is a triangular piece of land that juts into Taffa on its southern side. GFC and his descendants owned the point for a century, from 1920 to 2020; there was a camp on it till the mid-1960s.

cooking utensils, and hanging from one of the saplings were a score of odd-looking steel or iron contraptions, each attached to a length of chain.

The Indian paused in his task, and said in his low pleasant voice: "Pitch'm canoe. Catch musquash soon. Ice all melt two, t'ree day. Then trap him."

"Oh," cried Chris, "you trap? Tell me all about it, please."

The Indian picked up his pail, ran the stick through the handle and, going over, knelt and held it over the fire again. For a moment Chris stood abashed, thinking the man meant not to make any answer to the excited questions. But presently he looked up, a shrewd expression in his dark eyes as he said:

"Who you—who you fader? you?"

Chris explained. "You see," he added, "I'm new to this country and I do so want to learn everything I can!"

The Indian slowly nodded his chin. "I see," he said, "you what white man call green."

Chris nodded.

The Indian went on:

"I Noel Polchis.[6] Chief of Melicetes below Woodstock—" He pulled back his coat with his free hand, disclosing to the boy's view a star-shaped badge. Chris nodded again. This short, ill-clad Indian a chief! He had supposed that the chiefs at least would be more splendidly habited.

Noel Polchis continued, enumerating with slow deliberation:

"Me trap otter, mink, musquash, weasel, coon; everyt'ing. Last spring me trap big bear." He paused to wave his hand across the lake. "Over on Lawrence Peak. Sell him hide fifteen dollar." He ceased (the pitch in the tin pail was bubbling), rose and, stepping over to the canoe again, renewed his efforts to make the seams watertight.

---

6   His first name is pronounced "Noo-el". It rhymes with "jewel" not "Joel".

Chris, watching him, was thinking of some of his boy chums in the homeland; of how little, after all, they knew of conditions beyond their own island. And the books—how few depicted life in Canada as it actually was!

He would like—but of course he wouldn't dare ask such a favour—to watch Noel Polchis trap muskrats. He glanced at the lean-to again, then at the Indian.

"You camp—sleep here—nights? How jolly."

Noel Polchis deftly ran his pitching iron along the centre seam, finished, and answered:

"T'ree night. Me come down on train Friday from Woodstock. Stay two week." He paused, put down his utensils and said: "Me see if me catch'm trout. Come," and walked, followed by Chris, to the tip of the point. Bending, he rolled a stone from the end of an alder pole attached to a set line, picked it up gingerly, gave a tentative pull towards him, then, with "Me catch'm this time!" flung a fish far over his head.

With a shout of "You've got one. A whopper! A whopper!" Chris sprang backwards where the trout, a few feet from the fire, was flopping up and down.

Noel Polchis came forward, his black eyes sparkling, bent, ran his forefinger through the trout's gills and held it up for the boy's inspection. "Two pound," he muttered. "Fine trout. Me catch'm one for supper las' night."

He bent again, picked up a round stick, and tapping the trout on its head, put the beautiful thing out of its misery. Then he laid it down. "Bait'm hook; maybe catch more," he said, and going to the lean-to, came back in a moment with a small square of pork which he carefully put on the hook.

Chris's pulses were hammering. If he could only catch one of those beautiful speckled fish and take it home to his mother! But he wouldn't dare ask. This Indian doubtless wanted the few trout he could catch for his own use. Still, Noel, if he caught another, *might sell one.*

Chris bent and touched the rich carmine spots. "Oh," he said, "he's such a beauty. I never saw a live trout before in all my life."

Noel Polchis walked over and threw his baited hook into the water, close to the rim of ice, laid the pole on the ground, placed the stone securely on the handle, came back and said:

"You want him?"

"Oh," cried Chris, "want it—your fish? Why, I couldn't think of taking your trout. It wouldn't be right. You want it for dinner."

A faint smile played over the Indian's face. "You good boy," he said. "You take him. Me catch more by'm-by."

He drew a knife from his pocket, opened the blade, stepped to a young maple and cut off a forked branch, from which he deliberately whittled the small twigs. Then, bending, he passed one branch of the fork through the trout's gills and held it out to the boy. "Take him," he said.

For a moment Chris hesitated. The thought came to him that he should pay the Indian for this princely offering. But for some unexplainable reason he thought better of it. When he knew Noel Polchis more intimately, he was glad he hadn't offered him money.

With, "Thanks ever so," he took the trout from Noel's outstretched hand. He wanted to go at once and show his prize to his parents and Bob—Bob who would be as enthusiastic as any boy. And, too, he wanted to stay longer. He wanted to ask questions about the bark canoe, about trapping and hunting. He liked this Indian—this Noel Polchis—who was so human after all, so much more so than many whites. He hesitated a few minutes, watched Noel renew the fire and bend again over his pitch kettle. Then he said:

"May I—may I come again and talk with you?" he was about to add "Mr. Polchis," but after a moment's hesitation said: "Noel."

The Indian looked up. "You come," he said. "I show you how trap musquash. What they call you?"

For a second Chris was puzzled, then he understood.

"I'm Chris," he answered. "Chris Alison."

"Chris," repeated Noel in his musical voice. "Chris. Him good name. No know him, but good name all same."

He fumbled in his pocket, brought forth a short, black pipe and some odd-looking fragments that looked, thought Chris, for all the world like crinkly bits of very thin bacon, stuffed them into the bowl, struck a match, took a few puffs, then said: "Tobacco drop from pack on way out. Smoke alder bark."

"Oh," said Chris, "that's too bad." He had a swift vision of his father and Bob without their beloved weed, compelled to smoke alder bark as a substitute. The loss of Noel's tobacco was a real tragedy. "I'm so sorry," he said, and added: "Doesn't the bark bite your tongue, Noel; isn't it rather awful?"

The Indian shook his head. "Not bad. Sometimes smoke tea," and puffing away at his pipe he again began stirring the pitch in his black kettle.

Chris was thinking of the tins of smoking mixture in one of the boxes at home, and wondered if it was possible to beg one from his father or Bob to give to Noel. Despite the Indian's evident enjoyment of the alder bark, Chris was quite sure it must be but a poor substitute for genuine tobacco.

For a few minutes he silently watched Noel at his task, then, realising that there was much that required his presence at home, said:

"I must be going, Noel. Good-bye."

The Indian looked up. "*Adiou*," he said, his voice low, musical. "*Adiou*."

"What did you say, Noel?" asked Chris. Noel chuckled far down in his chest.

"*Adiou*," he repeated. "Him Injun; all same white man's good-bye."

"Oh," said Chris, "I see." Then he struck off happily through the trees from whence the brook—that had been responsible for this strange adventure—sent out its joyous little gurgles of errant laughter.

He walked on, swinging his trout by the forked stick and whistling a merry tune. And, as he walked, he saw two figures descending the road over the ridge. On he went. And presently, opposite the lane which led to Mr. Clowes' home, he came face to face with the two pedestrians. He felt his face grow hot. His eyes fastened for a brief moment on the school teacher's face. Then as she smiled at him and nodded he dared to glance at her companion. He was conscious of a twinkle in the hazel eyes, that the chin was set at a saucy angle. Then she said:

"I say, boy, you've had luck. Didn't know you English Johnnies could catch fish."

Abashed, he walked on. The cheek of her! Why shouldn't an English boy be capable of catching fish? And yet he hadn't caught it. He stopped, swung about. They were only a few yards away. He cried out:

"But I didn't catch it."

She turned her face over her shoulder, a thousand imps of mischief dancing in her eyes.

"Oh," she said, "you didn't? Found it hanging on a tree, perhaps."

He disdained a reply, and, as he turned and walked on, he heard, first a ripple of laughter, then the school teacher's voice reprovingly: "Winnie, you've been perfectly horrid."

His heart warmed to the older girl. She was a trump. He came opposite the dilapidated dwelling that was his new home, crossed the culvert, and in a few minutes was showing his fish and describing his adventures to his parents and Bob.

Chapter 4

The Pipe of Peace

It was morning, and the third since the coming of the immigrants to the ridge. It was raining; it had begun the afternoon before, continued throughout the night, ceased for a couple of hours after seven o'clock, and was now hard at it again.

The lad could hear his mother humming to herself in the other room. Bless her! Not a word of reproval or of regret that she had come to this out-of-the-way settlement to end her days. A pioneer? Yes, as Bob had proudly said to him, she too was a pioneer, uncomplaining; ready to do her bit towards making this land more solidly an Anglo-Saxon land.

They were to have a new house. Little thrills of excitement ran through the lad's body. A new house—a log bungalow of newly-peeled spruce logs from their own lot, down by the lake. Last evening, the family seated about the stove, the wind howling outside and the rain beating against the windows, Bob and Mr. Alison had talked it all over. Money was scarce. There were so many things to buy—farm implements, stock, horses—that it would be out of the question to purchase prepared lumber. In a few years, perhaps, if crops were good. But for the present, why not a clean, weather-tight dwelling of logs? Yes, they could do it. It wouldn't cost much. They'd ask Mr. Clowes' opinion and help.

And getting up, Bob had gone out in the rain towards the farm-house across the way, leaving Chris and his parents, the former dreaming dreams of paddling up the lake in Noel Polchis's canoe, and the latter planning a flower garden, with morning glories and zinnias and hollyhocks, as in the garden back home—in England.

An hour later Bob had come back, his jacket and cap wet with rain, but with shining eyes. Mr. Clowes had said it would be a very simple matter to get the logs and peel them. He'd come and help, and there was a carpenter chap over the other side of the ridge whom they could hire for a few days, if necessary. Two weeks would see the new house ready for occupancy. As soon as the logs were cut and hauled from the woods, they'd jack up the old building, drag it to one side to be used as a temporary dwelling, and lay the new house on the foundation of the old (beneath which was a very good stone-wall cellar). Bob had hastily sketched a rough plan of the new abode. It was to be one storey, with a big living- and dining-room combined, with two long windows facing the south; in the rear, overlooking the lake, three bedrooms; and on the east the kitchen.

The lad withdrew his eyes from the opposite hills, smiled to himself as he recollected how happy his mother was at the prospect (not that she wouldn't have shown a smiling face had they to put up with the present ramshackle abode). But he thought there was a new note to her song since yesterday.

He went over to a wooden peg by the south door, took down his rain-coat and cap, put them on, picked up a can of smoking mixture, which his father had generously consented that he present to Noel Polchis, and, opening the door of the main house, told his mother where he was going, listened to her caution that he do not get lost, and, bidding her not to worry, he'd be quite safe, went outdoors.

He turned and glanced at the forsaken highway, the brown road leading over the ridge towards Millville, up which he had watched his father and Bob and Mr. Clowes drive an hour before, to order windows for the living-room and bring back a load of boards and other necessaries.

How shut in from the outside world they were in this little valley! Three or four habitations, a school house perched on the top of the ridge—that was all. A few brown fields, and wilderness—no end. And yet he felt in high spirits this morning, splendid spirits. If the rain let up tomorrow he'd accompany the men down to the timber lot to cut down the trees for the log house. Perhaps he'd be allowed to help. In the meantime, ho, for a talk with Noel Polchis!

He ran down the hill, soggy with rain, crossed the fence, and coming to the woods, found the place where he had entered a couple of days before, and made straight for the singing brook. He smiled to himself as he thought of the treat in store for Noel, and remembered his father's words when, that morning before leaving, he had brought out the can of smoking mixture: "He'll likely prefer his alder bark, my boy." Oh no, Chris was quite sure Noel would like the mixture immensely.

There were the alder bushes beyond which he had scared the partridge from her nest. He decided to make a detour. It wouldn't do, he told himself, to disturb her often. He walked up the brook a few yards, leaped across, made a slight detour, then found the brook farther on. The bushes were drenched. The rain ran down his neck and his ankles were soon soaked, but he cared not. He was having a jolly lark. In five minutes he had reached the larger growth of trees, where it was easier travelling, and, breaking into a run, presently came to the point. Hurrah! Noel was home. Smoke was rising from a fire— though how anyone could keep a fire going in such a rain was amazing. In a few minutes he had reached the Indian's camp site.

As Chris stopped, the Indian looked up. Without removing the pipe from his mouth he said: "*Oolkiskak*."[7] Then, at Chris's, "How are you, Noel?" the Indian remarked in his low voice: "*Oolkiskak* all same fine day." Then, with a smile: "White man say fine day when rain, fine day when sun shine."

---

7   Later in the book GFC transcribes this Maliseet word as "*Illigiskit*".

Chris laughed. "Yes, that's true, Noel, we do. *Ool-kis-kak*," he repeated, "*oolkiskak*—fine day. I'll remember that, Noel, and *adiou* means good-bye, doesn't it?"

The Indian removed his pipe from his mouth, blew out a cloud of alder bark smoke, and a pleased look overspread his dark face. "Good," he said. "You Chris boy learn spik Injun quick. You stay—eat some of my trout?"

Chris glowed with pleasure. "Why, yes, Noel. I'll be very glad to," and sitting down beside Noel, he crossed his ankles and gazed into the leaping flames, at the smoke curling bravely upwards.

Said Noel: "Me trap fine musquash this morning at mouth of brook up there;" he pointed with his knife. "Fine skin. I show you by'm-by."

"Oh," cried Chris, "how jolly. You've got one already! How much is it worth, Noel?"

"Maybe one dollar, maybe dollar and a half," answered the Indian.

Chris restrained his desire to see the musquash skin at once, and said: "Noel, I found some pheasant's—or, as you call them here, partridge's—eggs that first day I saw you. Ten eggs, Noel, ten," he repeated jubilantly. "Just think, there'll be ten little partridges hatched out soon." The Indian nodded his chin gravely.

"Maybe," he answered slowly. "Maybe, if fox or owl don't get old mother hen," and gave his fish another turn.

"Oh," ejaculated Chris, "I never thought of that."

"Or bob-cat," went on Noel's low voice. "Partridge have hard life. Sometime bob-cat, sometime fox, sometime old owl get'm. Eat up eggs. No baby partridge. Too bad." With a satisfied nod he rose, swung his frying-pan from over the fire, said: "Him done; now you have some trout."

For many a day Chris Alison remembered that hour. The trout was excellent (Noel had cut it in half and given it to him on a tin plate). It savoured of wood smoke, but Chris didn't mind that. He was as happy and proud as a boy can be who has found his way into the heart of a son of the forest and been invited to share his trout fried in pork fat.

Noel said little. He ate quickly, and when finished set down his plate and picked up his pipe.

Then did Chris remove from his pocket the tin of smoking mixture, and, his heart drumming a little song of gladness, handed it to Noel with:

"I've brought you some real tobacco, Noel. I hope you'll like it."

A pleased smile spread over the Indian's face. "*To-ma-way?*"[8] he said. "You bring him to Noel?"[c]

Chris was nodding happily. "Let me show you how to open it, Noel," he cried. He took the can, opened his knife and ran the point of the blade through and around the label, along the edge of the cover. He knew that Noel was watching him with interest. He adjusted the little cutter, pressed it through the thin inner covering of tin, gave the cap a few quick turns, as he'd seen Bob do, and, removing both, passed the smoking mixture to Noel.

The Indian took it, held it to his nose a moment, then deliberately filled his pipe.

The boy watched fascinated, as, forcing the weed home with a brown forefinger, Noel struck a match and puffed rapidly until the tobacco was going nicely. A look of ineffable contentment passed over the Indian's face. The fragrant smoke curled above his head, mingled with the unnameable perfumes of the forest. For a few moments Noel spoke no word; but his silence, the enchanted look on his face as he inhaled and exhaled the smoke, was eloquent of his approval. At last he removed the pipe from his mouth and said:

"You good boy, Chris. Noel say thanks." And, as he put the stem between his lips again, he added, with a wave of his

---

8   Tobacco, a Maliseet word.

hand in a half-circle: "Some day I show you big woods. Show you moose, way up on bog where he come feed on lily roots. In October I show you how call him with birch bark horn. Hear him come grunt, grunt, like big hog. You shoot him. I show you how paddle canoe like Injun. You like that?"

"Oh, Noel," cried the boy, "like it? You don't know how much. You see, I'm going to live here on the ridge for many years, and I want to learn all I can about the forest and the animals." He paused, then added: "Mr. Bill Cummins says there are many deer over the lake on those wooded ridges."

Noel gave a low grunt. "White man take gun and go shoot deer. Walk fast, scare all game; no get shot. Travel five, eight, ten mile. Run all over woods. See no game. Come home night all tired; no deer. Injun go up on ridge, sit down, wait long time. No deer come. Wait some more. By'm-by see doe deer feedin' on beech nuts on ground. No shoot; want big buck. By'm-by see something move. Maybe wind blow leaf off tree. No take'm eyes off dat spot; just look and p'r'aps cock gun. Pretty soon see big buck come from behind tree. Den shoot. *Kadama!*"

He ceased suddenly, turned his eyes from the boy's eager face and with his head on one side, his dark eyes on the forest to his right, sat immovable, listening.

Presently a bush cracked, then the "tump, tump" of approaching footsteps fell on Chris's ear, and a moment later a man past middle age, with a pack on his back, emerged from the forest. He came on with short, quick steps, gave the Indian a brusque "How do, Noel?" flashed a glance at the boy and, slipping the straps of the pack from his shoulders, laid it on the ground, sat himself down, filled and lighted his pipe. When it was going nicely he turned to Noel and said: "They told me out at the station you were here."

Noel made no reply. He had relighted his pipe and was puffing away serenely, his eyes on the newcomer. The man went on: "Where's Gabe Joe?"

The Indian gave him a shrewd glance. "Gabe Joe—he over Trout Lake,"[d] he said in a careless voice.

"Oh," said the man. "Sure he didn't go to the beaver dam on the Keswick?"

A frown passed over the Indian's face. He said: "Maybe yes; maybe no. Gabe say he go Trout Lake," with which Noel tapped the ashes from his pipe and slowly refilled it from the tin of smoking mixture at his side.

The man made no comment for several moments. He opened his pack, drew out a flat round can, removed the top and methodically began to smear some of the contents on the soles and along the seams of his moccasins. At length he looked over at Noel and said:

"I've got to keep my eyes on you chaps this year. Last spring ten beaver were taken from the Brandon meadows and smuggled over into the States. Personally I don't care how many skins get by the United States Customs men, but my business is to see that no beaver are taken illegally. You get me, Noel? If you want beaver you got to first buy the tags from the Government. Four dollars for each tag. And no deer shot out of season, Noel, you understand?"

The Indian slowly nodded, removed his pipe, put it in his pocket and said:

"Noel Polchis learn to read when he boy. No forget. He read game law. You boil the kittle, John?"

The other shook his head. "Thanks," he said. "I dinnered at Jordan's on the ridge." He put the grease can in his pack, cleaned out his pipe, refilled, lighted it and puffed away in silence for some moments. At length, whether because of its soothing influence or Noel's invitation for him to take lunch, he began speaking, and his voice was entirely lacking its previous brusqueness, was indeed comradely, a trifle sad:

"The old pine is gone at last, Noel," he said. "Perkins cut it down as he threatened to."

Noel Polchis gave a single, low exclamation.

"Yes, last week," went on the man. "It was hollow in the butt; but even so it scaled eighteen hundred feet of boards." He ceased a moment, then added grimly: "Perkins was satisfied."

Again there was silence, save for the crackling of the fire and the soft beat of the rain on the tarpaulin above their heads. Then the man called John went on:

"That tree was a thousand years old, Noel. I never went up the valley without stopping and taking off my hat to it in homage. A thousand years, Noel, it had graced that hillside, had withstood all the anger of the elements. The wind had carried its seed far and wide to reforest the soil. It was there hundreds of years ago, before your forefathers dreamed there was such an animal as the white man. High above its fellows it watched the boats of the first settlers coming up the river. I say *watched*, Noel, for who can say trees have not some power of sight? And then along comes Perkins with the soul of a louse and lays the monarch low." The man ceased again, and puffed away thoughtfully at his pipe. At last: "I felt as though I had lost a friend—an old friend."

While he had been talking the boy had felt his heart go out to him with a sudden rush. He understood so well what the other had, in his recital of the passing of the big pine, perhaps unwittingly betrayed—an intense love of the woods, of nature. Regretfully he saw the big man rise, slip the straps of his pack over his shoulders.

"Good-bye, Noel," he said. Chris felt the keen grey eyes on him, then: "And good-bye, you—what's *your* name?"

Chris replied: "My name's Alison—Chris Alison. We came here from England and settled on the White farm;" and, politely: "May I ask your name?"

A smile passed over the man's face. "Oh yes," he answered. "Turn about's fair play. My name's Richardson—John Richardson. I'm the game warden and fire ranger for this county." He paused, added thoughtfully: "So you're English—Well, good-bye. *Adiou,* Noel." And turning, he walked off.

For several moments Chris watched him threading the trees around the little bay that formed the eastern boundary of the lake. Then he was awakened by Noel's voice:

"John Richardson good woodsman, he good canoeman." He paused a moment, added: "Injun don't like white man say, 'Don't do this. Don't do that.' Before white man come, Injun own all this woods, rivers, lakes. Now white man say, 'Don't spear salmon. Don't shoot deer and moose.' Give Injun little piece land. Say, 'live here.' If he want beaver, pay Gov'ment four dollar for tag. Maybe no get beaver. If he want shoot deer or moose, pay Gov'ment three dollar for licence." He paused again, gazed, his eyes wide, sadly off through the trees, nor spoke for some time. And in perhaps no better way than this visit of the game warden and fire ranger to his friend could Chris have had impressed upon him the forest law of the land, as well as the sense of injustice with which the natives of the soil viewed the decree of their white conquerors. He felt that he should say something to make his companion feel better, yet knew not how to begin. Noel sat, his pipe out, the stem held listlessly between his brown fingers, his eyes brooding. The boy reached out, timidly touched his arm, and said:

"Noel, you promised to show me the musquash skin—you remember?"

Slowly the Indian withdrew his eyes from the forest, and rising, said:

"Come. I show you."

Chapter 5

Forest Lore

It rained steadily for five days, and broke up the remaining ice left in the lake. After the rain had ceased, Chris followed the men down to the timber block and, though at first only an interested spectator, soon found himself taking an active part in getting out the logs for the new dwelling. Besides his father and Bob, were Mr. Clowes and his son, Sidney.

Sid, as everyone on the Ridge—save Miss Allen, the teacher—called him, was a sturdy brown-eyed lad, Chris's own age, but with muscles hard as iron. He wore long trousers, like a man,[9] wore a felt hat tilted at a rakish angle, could chop down a tree as well as most men, steer a course through the woods to almost any desired point, and had already killed two buck-deer. Behind a team of horses, his tanned fists knotted about the plough handles, he could run a tolerably straight furrow; was strong enough to manipulate the levers on the reaper and raking machines; knew considerable veterinary lore; and despite all these accomplishments was not a bit boastful. If you had complimented him on his abilities he would doubtless have said: "Shucks! Any of the boys around here can do the same." And indeed it would have been no more than the truth, so far as farm craft is concerned. The instinct that guides one through pathless forests—this is the heritage of your true woodsman, a gift rather than something acquired. And of this Sid would surely have said: "Oh, it's quite easy."

---

9   In the 1910s and 1920s most boys wore short trousers—to the knee or just above—till they were thirteen or fourteen.

Though the friendship between the two lads was of only a few days' standing, it was already firmly cemented. Each had found something to admire in the other: Chris the ready friendliness of the Canadian boy; the latter, the boy-of-the-world air of the English lad, who had seen and could tell so entertainingly of far places.

Down in the timber block Chris stood and awesomely watched Sid, armed with a double-bitted axe, step up to a big spruce tree; with a few quick strokes cut away any small bushes that might foul his back stroke. Then, spitting on his brown palms, Sid would swing the axe about his head, to bury its bright blade deep in the soft, juicy wood. How the chips flew, and the sound of the chopping echoed throughout the wood. Having made a deep V-shaped notch in the trunk, a few feet from the ground, Sid began about six inches higher, cutting downward to the V, widening and deepening it. Now on the opposite side of the tree, a little above the first cutting, Sid began, with each blow of his axe emitting a short grunt. At last the tree quivered, swayed, and with a word of caution to Chris to stand back and to one side, Sid pressed one shoulder against the towering monster and, as it toppled over, sprang quickly to one side so that, should the trunk bound backward, he would be out of danger. As, with a crash, the great spruce tore its way to earth and lay still, Sid, giving vent to a triumphant shout, would leap at it and begin to lop off its branches.

Watching his Canadian friend this first morning, Chris flung out question after question. Why Sid did this or that; how many years were required to produce a merchantable log; what were the different qualities of spruce, fir, maple, birch, hemlock, ash; what was the value in dollars and cents of each? All of which, Sid, between chopping and grunts, answered.

Chris's brain did some rapid mental arithmetic. Why, on their own land they had many hundreds of dollars' worth of timber! He thought of those silent ridges across the lake, that stretched, unbroken, many, many miles; those countless trees through which the train had wound its way only a few days ago! What a heritage, what a treasure the people of this Canada possessed!

After dinner that day he carried back to the woods with him a small axe which Sid generously loaned, and, long after painful blisters appeared on his hands, he persisted in lopping off the branches of the trees. He joyed in the labour, in the feeling that in his small way he was helping to prepare timbers for the new house. He liked the smell of the resinous wood and, above all, the informing comradeship of the lad who worked beside him. And, sensing Sid's hunger for knowledge of seas and distant places, he in turn gave generously. It seemed incredible that Sid (save once when he had gone with his father to Fredericton on the train) had never been farther than the village of Millville, had lived all his life here in the valley between the ridges, had few acquaintances outside the limits of Millville.[10]

For two days they worked at cutting down and lopping off the branches of the trees. Then the horses and low wagons were brought down and the logs were loaded on and hauled up to the door-yard. Now the bark was removed. Then they were sawed with a long cross-cut saw to the required lengths, and the ends were dovetailed, so that when one log was set upon the other they were not only bound firmly, but left only tiny crevices which later could be "chinked" with moss.

How quickly the four walls rose! Then came the long stringers, and the work on the gently-sloping roof began. Often Mrs. Alison came out of the old weather-stained dwelling— now reposing a few rods from the stone foundation on which it formerly sat—and smilingly gazed on the freshly peeled logs that were to be her new home. She said little—it being her staid, British manner; but Chris knew that though at times she must

---

10 Like a man named John Noel, with whom GFC used to go hunting. He lived on Howland Ridge and had never been further from home than Millville.

long for the friendships of the old land, she was determined that she would not be the one to discourage her men-folk.

One day he drove out with Bob to Millville for a load of shingles, the new windows, some beaver board[11]—with which the interior was to be faced—and some paint. On the way back, as they passed the schoolhouse, the teacher and Winnie Clowes came out. Bob pulled up his horses and gave them a ride down the hill. And as they rode, Winnie Clowes, seated beside Chris on the rear of the high wagon, commented on the new house, said it would be fine (he would have preferred "jolly") to live there. So clean and smelly, like the woods. She seemed to the boy so much more human—less like a spoiled, wilful child— than on previous occasions.

She said, "Can you shoot?" and added before he could reply, "I can. I went out with Dad last fall and helped to shoot a deer; three points on a side. And I've shot partridge. Do you like the woods?"

He nodded. "Immensely," he said.

"I know the trail over the ridge to the Keswick," she went on. "There's lots of trout in the Keswick." She paused, flashed him a quick look, and he wondered if she remembered the day she had been so discourteous about the trout Noel Polchis had given him. She did, for she said: "Not as big as the one you had the other day, but they're good pan trout, just the right size for eating."

They had reached the foot of the hill and were opposite the new house, the roof boarded and ready for the shingles. As Bob brought the horses to a stop, the girl said:

"On the 24th of May[12] I'll get my brother Sid and Miss Allen and we'll go over to the river and catch some trout. That is—"

---

11 Wood fibre compressed into sheets [Wikipedia].

12 The 24th of May was Queen Victoria's birthday. Victoria Day has been a public holiday in Canada since 1845.

she flashed him a saucy look from her brown eyes, "if you aren't afraid we'll lose you."

"Why, of course. Yes," he said. "That would be jolly. I'd love to go."

She had slipped nimbly to the ground. "That would be jolly," she mimicked his voice, adding in an undertone, an impish smile curving her lips: "You English all say 'jolly', don't you, and, 'yes, by Jove'?"

He stared at her a moment in silence, then, "Rather," he replied, at which she giggled outright.

She stood watching him until the team had started, then linked her arm within Miss Allen's.

"What an odd girl," thought Chris. And yet—she *was* rather a jolly sort, too.

He had little time to himself those days. There was so much to do; water to be carried from the spring, the cow—which had been purchased from Mr. Clowes—to milk, wood to split, the soil in the weed-clogged garden to be prepared for seeds; beds dug up in front of the house for the flower garden and fertilised with manure. In fact he was so busy that only twice—once in company with Bob after supper—did he have a chance to visit Noel Polchis.

He found that Noel was daily adding to his muskrat pelts. He had now fifty skins stretched on pieces of wood, and before the season ended he hoped to have as many more. This was vastly interesting. As he worked, the boy often saw Noel paddling his bark canoe up the lake and through the thoroughfare,ᵉ sometimes to turn off to his right and worm a circuitous course up the winding brook, across the small barren, that, a mile farther on, merged in a low lying growth of thick evergreens—the vanguard of those forest-clad ridges of oak and ash and beech and spruce that stretched on and on into the remote distance.

Up that brook, one evening, Noel took the boy in his canoe, the Indian using his paddle so skilfully, never once lifting the blade from the water, that it seemed to Chris as though the canoe was moving of its own volition. Noel described his method as feathering the paddle. Chris, who was in the centre of the canoe, facing the bow, turned his head and watched Noel's motions. He saw the paddle blade quickly but silently turn in the water, take a forward motion, its thin edge on a line with the canoe, then turn to form an angle and, obeying the strong muscles of the paddler, sweep sternward, to send the light craft bounding over the water.

The declining sun shone warm and bright, and, as they went, Noel's low voice drew attention to things which, until now, Chris had never seen or heard of. Those blades of grass pushing their heads above the surface of the water, the wild duck fed on. Those bushes along the bank—Labrador tea; that deformed looking tree—a tamarack. Once Noel stopped, reached out and plucked from the brook's margin an odd-looking plant, which he said was the pitcher plant. Farther on, floating in a little bay, was something which reminded the boy of a banana stock. Noel said it was a lily root, which a moose had pulled up from the muddy bottom of the brook the preceding fall. Once, as they rounded a bend, a long-legged bird rose and, with a great flapping of its broad wings and emitting a strange cry, went sailing over the barren towards the green timber. "A crane," said Noel. "He stand in water and watch with his little sharp eyes until he see fish come by, then he make one dart with his bill. All over; gobble him down. Den he stand dere lookin' like old stump stickin' outa water till 'nodder fish come 'long."

Every few yards he stopped to look at his traps, some set cunningly in little houses or pens made of sticks, others on short lengths of log secured to the bank. Twice, with a low grunt of satisfaction, he lifted out a trap with a drowned muskrat firmly caught in the steel jaws. Once he found a trap sprung, and with, "Noel catch'm next time," reset it, more carefully. Farther on, where the brook narrowed, a deer stood, calmly surveyed them a moment, then, with a wild leap and a snort that startled the boy, rushed like the wind across the barren and disappeared in the woods. For several moments, until distance swallowed the sound, they could hear it emitting those terrified snorts—"whistles" Noel called them.

"By'm-by when it get warm, big moose come here feed," he said. "Mudder moose bring calf. Stay near alders. When bull come along, he ugly. Horns in velvet, flies bodder him. Cow she take calf moose in thick alders. Hide him."

And thus Noel talked, describing the habits of the forest creatures, the boy listening spellbound. It was all so new, so strange. He hated to think of Noel going back to Woodstock; for he was, in a week or ten days. The season for trapping would be over. But there were a wife and a son and three daughters back there on the reservation, and, as Noel said, he must make baskets during the summer months. Half-bushel baskets to sell to the farmers, and fancy baskets of sweet hay for the women of the town. "But," assured Noel, "I come back in October. I show you how hunt deer, call big bull moose, sure. I come."

"You won't forget, Noel," pleaded Chris. The Indian shook his head. "I no forget," he said, and turned the canoe.

As they emerged from the brook into the lake again, a flock of black ducks rose and flew to the foot of the lake, where they settled and began to feed again.

"In September," said Noel, "season for duck open. Den you have roast duck for eat."

"Yes," said Chris. "Bob has a shot-gun, double barrelled."

"I tell you," said Noel, "you make boat. Come up in thoroughfare or brook, pull up boat on bog. Wait till duck come 'long. Den shoot. No use chase 'em over lake. They fly."

He paddled on, reached the centre of the lake, then spoke again.

"Chris, you see dat log straight ahead stickin' out water?[13] Dat spring-hole. When July come big trout go there. Noel know. White man fish all over lake; no get trout. You tie boat to dat log, then fish; put grasshopper on hook; maybe he won't bite; try fly. You get 'im in Millville. No fish middle of day. Trout lazy. After six o'clock try'm. Den they feed."

Chris tried to express his gratitude. "Thanks; thank you a thousand times, Noel," he cried. "I'll try not to forget all the things you've told me."

Noel said nothing in reply. He turned the canoe shoreward, opposite the log house, on the new roof of which the setting sun was casting its warm rays.

Noel brought his canoe close to the rocky beach, got out, and holding on to the gunwale, steadied the frail craft for Chris to disembark.

"You no get scared," he said. "You catch hold of gunwale with both hands; then you get up, slow. Never mind canoe rock, den step out, first one foot, den other. That's right. You no shove canoe out in lake like sport I take moose-huntin' on Miramichi. He shoot'm big bull from canoe, an' I paddle him to shore. I tell him be careful. What he do?" Noel gave a snort of disgust. "He jump out; upset canoe. Blankets all wet, grub all wet. Den he look at me and say: 'You, Injun, why you not steady canoe?'" Noel ceased, picked up his paddle from the beach, stepped carefully into the stern of his canoe, said, "Good-bye Chris," and, standing up, one foot slightly advanced ahead of the other, his knees bending with each stroke of his paddle, he drove his craft along the shore towards his camp site.

Chris watched him a few moments, envied the perfect ease with which Noel stood up and paddled, wondered if he

---

13 The old log is a big rampike stuck at an angle in one of the deepest places in the lake, about halfway across from the point. It was there when GFC first saw Taffa, in 1920, and a hundred years later, in 2020, it is still there.

would soon be able to perform such a feat. Then he climbed the bank, pushed through a narrow strip of second growth poplar and maples to the field beyond, and broke into a trot towards home.

As he ran he was building, in fancy, a board boat, with the aid of Bob, and had made up his mind to ask Noel to make him a couple of paddles.

As he reached the house, Bob raised his dripping face from a wash-pan standing on a low bench beside the door, grinned, and said:

"Hello, youngster; had a good time?"

Chris gave him a quick look. There was no envy on Bob's face, only little tired lines. His conscience smote him. While he had been having the time of his life with Noel, Bob was working, doing odd jobs which *he* might have very well done. He said in a low voice:

"I've had such a jolly time, Bob," and then, promptly forgetting his momentary conscience prick, launched into an enthusiastic account of his trip with Noel.

"That's all splendid," said Bob. "Yes, lad, we'll try to get time to build the boat. But," he glanced about him, "there's so much to do. Tomorrow we're to start ploughing. While you were away Mr. Simmons brought the horses."

"The horses—oh, Bob, may I see them now?" cried Chris.

Bob smiled good-naturedly. "Come," he said; and led the way to the barn.

He opened the stable door and Chris, gazing into the darkened stalls, saw a grey and a black, feeding contentedly. He walked in, ran his hand along their warm necks, gave each a gentle pat and came out, his eyes shining.

"It seems more like home to have them," he said, and accompanied Bob back to the house.

The sun had gone down. The western sky was crimson. The lake's bosom mirrored its glory. Soon dark would fall.

Suddenly, from the very heart of the water, it seemed, a cry arose, prolonged, maniacal in its mocking intensity.

The boy shivered, looked up into his brother's face. "What is it?" he asked in awed tones.

Bob laughed. "It's a loon," he said. "A silly loon. Its cry or laugh—whichever it is—is weird, I admit. I saw and heard one some years ago, in Scotland. It took a rise out of me." He put his hand affectionately on Chris's shoulder. "Come, laddie, early to bed. We have much to do tomorrow."

Chapter 6

Work

The ground was covered with sparkling frost when, having dressed, Chris ran down to the spring to fetch a pail of water. He dipped up a pail full, set it down, and for a moment or two stood watching the water boiling up from the sandy depths; then he knelt on the board beside the spring, put out his hands, allowed his body to sink to a level with the water and putting down his mouth drew in deep draughts. Oh, it was good; the sweetest, purest water he had ever tasted.

He rose, picked up his pail and, whistling, went back to the house.

His mother met him at the kitchen door. She smiled into his eyes, said: "You're happy here, aren't you, Chris?"

He nodded.

"So am I," she said: "I never thought I could be. But it's really *home* to me now."

She went in and he set the pail of water on the bench, picked up the milking pail and went to the barn.

As he milked he heard Bob whistling in the adjoining stable; heard one of the horses whinny for its oats. From the henhouse came the sudden cackling of a hen. The boy's imagination pictured a new-laid egg in one of the straw nests. In two more weeks the old hen which he and his mother had put the eggs under would be off the nest, and hatching a new brood of chicks. He hoped for good luck. And thinking of the sitting hen his fancy flew to the mother partridge by the old log near the brook. Doubtless—if a bob-cat or an owl or a fox hadn't got her— she was already leading her wild brood over the wooded slope beside the laughing brook. And thinking of the brook led him to think of fishing; because a girl his own age had asked him to go trouting in May. His fancy slipped across the highway to Winnie Clowes and the school teacher. And he remembered his mother's whispered words of a few nights before to the effect that "She liked the teacher very much and what a sweet capable wife she would make Bob."

He rose, gave the cow's flank a parting pat, and went back to the house, where he found breakfast waiting.

It was the first breakfast in the new house. The cloth was spread on the deal table, which Mr. Alison had made. A heaping dish of buckwheat pancakes—the meal had been given Mrs. Alison by Mrs. Clowes—buttered and covered with syrup— purchased from Porter, who lived in the last house on the ridge—made a new and most palatable breakfast.

"We won't have to buy syrup next year," said Mr. Alison. "Porter says we've one of the finest maple groves in the settlement, and all we have to do is to tap the trees, collect the sap and boil it down. Any that we don't need for our own use we can sell. Of course," continued Mr. Alison to Bob, "it's not quite so simple as Porter says. There must be something beyond mere chance in the successful making of maple syrup. But Porter says he'll gladly show us how it's done."

Said Mrs. Alison: "We've been here only a little more than three weeks and we've met with nothing but kindness from our neighbours. I hope I shall never forget it."

"As you've said, Mother, one mustn't forget the kindness shown us by our neighbours. We can never repay them save by trying to understand their point of view and dwelling beside them in friendship."

Chris said nothing, though sponge-like he was absorbing all that was said. He heartily agreed with his parents. He would take all the inhabitants of the ridge into his heart—with one exception. Neither Bob nor his father had been a witness to a piece of Canadian intolerance and ill-manners as personified in Miss Winnie Clowes. Had she not slightingly spoken of them as English Johnnies that first day at Millville, and again twitted him about being an English greeny the day Noel gave him the trout? Of course, an inner voice defended, she was but a child, only twelve, and she had partly atoned by asking him to go trout fishing the 24th of May. But then, too, had she not spoiled things by assuming that he might possibly be afraid she and her brother would lose him in the woods? Grown-ups and her brother Sid were different, quite; but this girl was shockingly discourteous and careless of a strange boy's feelings.

He finished his breakfast, sat in silence until the others rose, then he brought another pail of water from the spring, filled the space behind the stove with wood, and went to the barn where Bob and his father had gone to harness the horses preparatory to ploughing.

On this and for several days following he trudged back and forth the length of the field, guiding the horses, while Bob held the plough handles. As the days grew warmer the work became more arduous. Then came the harrowing, and as he followed the unwieldy thing back and forth, back and forth, the sweat trickled from his brow into his eyes, his cheeks burned; bits of soil and gravel worked into his shoes, bruised his feet. So tired and leg-weary he was that, after the evening meal, he went about the chores as one in a dream, and immediately his aching body struck the bed he was fast asleep.

One morning, as he worked, he was suddenly conscious of someone standing beside him, and looking up saw that it was Noel, his pack strapped on his back, a bundle of skins beneath one arm, and two new paddles in his free hand. He said: "I go Woodstock to-day. I make'm paddles. Sprucewood. They light. Good-bye. I come huntin' season, sure."

"But," cried Chris, "how much, Noel?—how much am I to pay you for the paddles?"

The Indian smiled, and said: "Noel no take money from friend." Then, at the lad's stammered thanks, held out his hand. "*Adiou*, Chris," he said. "Train come Millville ten o'clock. I leave paddles at barn." He wrung the boy's hand, turned, and hastily moved away.

With an odd feeling about his heart Chris watched him top the rise of ground and disappear, then he resumed his harrowing to where Bob, at the other end of the field, was waiting to relieve him.

By the middle of the following week they had their grain all in and a field prepared for potatoes, turnips and a patch of buckwheat, and the garden plot ploughed, harrowed, and fertilised with some old manure that had been lying behind the barn when they came. Then Chris, under his mother's guidance, prepared beds for lettuce, cucumbers, squash, pumpkins; long rows for peas, beans, onions; and short rows for summer savory and sage. They were surprised to find that few farmers on the ridge paid much attention to vegetable culture. For excuse was given lack of time—fields of grain and hay and potatoes were of far greater importance. But as Chris's mother remarked, green vegetables, in season, were also important as well as necessary. Besides, she'd be lost without her garden.

Often Chris paused in his labour to glance at the lake and the surrounding hills, and long for a boat and fishing tackle that he might try for trout, or ramble over the forest. But there was no time for such pleasure now. His back might ache to breaking point, his hands blister from spading and raking and hoeing. Mosquitoes came from the forest and swamp and annoyed him frightfully, raising rounded weals on his wrists, neck, and forehead that itched painfully. And thus, one morning, he wondered, in his boy's soul, why people endured all this toil when there was easier work to do in the world. Here he was, the sweat streaming down his face, his boots browned with the soil, his hands blistered, his body too tired to read after the evening chores.

Why had Bob, his father and mother, having worked all their lives farming in England, come to this isolated valley rather than seek work in a city? What was their future here? Why had Mr. Clowes' father come over the ridge to this, at the time, a mere wilderness, to make a home for himself and family and plant his first crop between the blackened tree trunks? For the moment, being very young and excessively tired, he could think of no reason for this madness of grown men.

But presently to him came the old spirit of the pioneer, who dares great hardships, performs enormous toil that civilisation may expand, that the hungry in cities may be nourished. And a little breeze suddenly sprang up, bearing from the forest innumerable perfumes of bursting buds on maple and birch and alder, of wild flowers in damp nooks, trailing arbutus, anemone, hepatica, the resinous odour of spruce and fir. He straightened his aching back, drew in a deep draught of the scented wind. A robin from one of the gnarled apple trees in the straggly orchard piping up a gladsome melody struck a responsive chord in the lad's soul. He puckered his lips and mimicked the red-breasted songster. He felt better. There was work to do, yes; plenty of it, but when the crops were all in there would be time for play—rambles over those wooded ridges, paddling in the boat (which Bob had promised to build) and then in the autumn, hunting. And in the winter would there not be skating, sliding, and snowshoeing and skiing? No, he mustn't complain of his work. Again he thought of Mr. Clowes' father coming over the ridge to make a home in the wilderness. Yes, such as he were the real pioneers. Should he, Chris Alison, whine, find fault with conditions as they now were? For comparison, he imagined his parents, Bob and himself, going to a spot such as one of those wooded ridges across the lake, cutting down trees to make space for a home, clearing the soil of roots and rocks and fallen brush. His eyes dwelt on the brown fields stretching on either side of him, ploughed, harrowed, seeded, awaiting the sun's rays and the kindly rain. Glorious! No, he mustn't grumble, or he would actually merit the scorn of such as Winnie Clowes, of her brother Sid, who even now was teaming his horses over the slope of yonder hill.

His mother came out, with packets of seed in a small basket, bent and carefully placed them one by one in the little runlets he had prepared. As they worked, side by side, she talked to him, not of England, but of this new land, of her joy in the new house, her plans for a summer porch screened against the flies and mosquitoes where they could sit evenings and Sundays and read. With sweet hopeful words she pictured the future: herds of cattle and sheep in the pastures, the barns enlarged, possibly an addition to the log house. It seemed to the boy as though she were conscious of the late turmoil in his heart. He wondered.... And felt ashamed of himself.

She spoke of Bob and the school teacher across the way. "She is so sensible, so sweet and modest. She would make him a splendid wife," she said.

And meanwhile, up the succession of hills leading from Millville to the ridge, Bob was driving his team of horses with a load of fertiliser for the potato field.

Another week of labour followed, with Chris sitting on the doorstep beside his father and mother cutting up the seed potatoes. As soon as a basket was filled it was placed on a wheelbarrow, and the boy trundled it across the field to where Bob was dropping them in the prepared rows. Another year they hoped to have a planter—a horse-drawn affair that automatically dropped the seed and covered it with fertiliser and earth. It was astonishing how things were done in this country—how much labour-saving machinery was used. As Bob said, these Canadians had the right idea, and it was silly to cling to old methods a bit longer than lack of funds made necessary.

When the potatoes were all in, the quarter acre flanking the timber lot was sown with turnip seed. And now Chris hoped that Bob would have time to begin the construction of the boat. But not yet. Down they went with axes and saws to the timber lot, where for a week they cut and sawed at maple and birch and hauled it up to the house for firewood.

The trees were entirely leaved out. The grass in the pasture was a rich green. In the woods the trillium, blood-root, hepatica and adder's tongue magically bloomed; and in the meadow grass and along the overflow from the spring Chris had already found a few purple violets (a week later there were myriads of them). In the evenings frogs whistled down in the marsh, a continuous chorus, occasionally half-drowned by the deep bass of some grandfather frog's chug-a-rum! chug-a-rum!

The days grew much warmer. Several times that month during the night it rained, and in the morning the face of nature looked clean and refreshed. Often in the evenings Mr. Clowes, with his family and the teacher, came over and sat either in the big living-room, through the screened doors of which only an occasional mosquito penetrated, or in the yard outside in the lee of a small fire (called a smudge) which burned in a large iron kettle, the smoke from which kept away insects. During these visits the men talked farming; the women of household duties, exchanging receipts for cake or bread or biscuits, discussed the making of butter, cheese, the raising of turkeys, geese; the proper way to pack eggs for winter use.

At last, much to Chris's delight, Bob began work on the board boat. They had a willing helper in Sid Clowes, and in about a day and a half the craft was ready for a first coat of paint. The hours it took to dry seemed interminable to Chris; but at length it was ready for the second painting. This, one evening, was nearly completed when the lad noted his brother suddenly cease and look towards the house, saw a flush spread over the tanned cheeks. Following his glance Chris saw the Clowes, accompanied by the teacher, in the act of entering the house. At Bob's: "We'll leave the rest of the painting until morning, son," he regretfully laid down his brush and followed Bob to greet the visitors.

That evening, just about dark, a thunderstorm came up from the north-west. It came suddenly, gave little warning of its approach. The first intimation that a storm was imminent was a blinding flash that lighted up the half-darkened room and sent the visitors to their feet. Mr. Alison and his wife begged them to stay until it was over, but there was no restraining them. As Mr. Clowes said, his place was home. Lightning might strike his barns, and there would be the stock to get out, and the farm machinery. "You never know," he added, "what might happen." On her way to the door Winnie Clowes passed Chris and stopped to whisper, "You ain't afraid of thunderstorms, are you?"

He shook his head, disdaining a verbal reply to this bobbed-haired elf. He noted that Bob had left the house. Going to the window he saw his brother walking beside Miss Allen down the lane. At this moment there came another deafening clap of thunder, a dash of rain against the window. He saw Bob tear off his jacket and fling it about the teacher's shoulders. Then the road was blotted out in a perfect deluge of rain. The lad turned. His father was placidly smoking his pipe, his mother, rocking back and forth in her chair, had resumed her knitting of a jersey she was doing for Bob.

Chris walked into his own bedroom and, standing by the window, gazed awesomely at the chains of fire that darted from the sky, lighting up the ridges from west to north and east, lighting up the surface of the lake, wave tossed, rain driven. He heard his parents talking in the other room, his mother's anxious voice saying that Bob would be soaked to the skin, that she must get him a dry shirt ready; her hopes that no farmer would have his buildings struck this night. The boy thought of the forest creatures: the deer and moose, the winged things; wondered if the storm terrified them. What an awful night for even a wild animal to be out in. Suddenly, directly across the lake, he saw a bolt of flame descend, heard a mighty crash that seemed to shake the world, the very house in which he stood. He closed his eyes, for the flash had almost blinded him. He heard a little cry from his mother, turned, saw the door open and Bob enter, the water running from him in streams. The boy was only dimly conscious of the conversation that followed, for his face was pressed against the window, his eyes staring into the night. Above the beating of the rain he could hear, far off on those opposite ridges and in their own wood lot nearer at hand, a steady roaring sound like a battling host; with every few minutes a crash as some giant tree came tearing to the ground. When the lightning flashed, he could see every object in the door-yard and in the fields, far-off Lawrence Peak and the vast wilderness of the Keswick Valley.

Presently the storm passed eastward. As it abated, he could hear the dull mutterings of distant thunder, as of a disgruntled monster retreating, and soon, over Lawrence Peak, a star twinkled like a friendly lamp in the blue. The wind fell; the rain ceased. From the eaves of the house, he could hear the water drip, falling with a tinkling sound in the puddle below.

Chapter 7

Coxswain Chris

Two days later they put the boat on the low farm wagon, hauled it down to the lake shore and launched it. Chris was in high spirits. This flat-bottomed, sixteen-foot boat was, to him, a marvel of workmanship. The bow and stern had been decked over, the latter forming a seat for the steersman. A six-inch board amidships and one nearer the bow made seating accommodation for at least five passengers. It drew, possibly, a trifle less than three inches of water, and, to the brothers' delight, leaked very little. A few days in the water would swell the bottom boards so that they would be quite tight.

Bob took the stern, Chris the bow seat, and they paddled out into the lake. And now each was to realise that the art of paddling, and at the same time keeping the craft straight, was not such a simple performance as it had seemed to be when watching Noel Polchis in his bark canoe. With all their efforts to keep it straight the boat swung about, first to the right, now to the left, describing short half-circles—like the needle of an unstable compass. After fifteen minutes of hard labour, Chris swung about, gazed at Bob's flushed and perspiring face, grinned and said:

"I say, old chap, we haven't gone fifty yards."

Bob rested his paddle, looked back at the shore, and turning muttered: "About that, youngster. At the rate we're going we'll reach the brook some time about nightfall." He pulled out his handkerchief and mopped his brow.

"I say," said Chris, "I'll be coxswain of this craft for a while. I know how Noel performed."

"Go ahead then, coxy," said Bob. "Anything to keep us from going in a circle. Makes one sea-sick."

Chris grinned happily. "Should have brought a supply of patent pills along," he remarked jocularly. He swung about, facing Bob. "Now," he said, "put your paddle blade in the water, draw it along the side of the boat—that's it—only don't wear the handle off against the gunwale. Now, turn the blade away from you, like a rudder, holding it so a moment. That's it. Splendid, Bob. Now again. Not so bad. We went three feet that stroke," and the lad laughed heartily.

Thus, for a half-hour, between laughter and jest, Chris coached and Bob performed, and they had crossed the lake. Now Chris took his own paddle and helped, although at times he found it necessary to paddle on the opposite side from Bob to assist in keeping the boat straight.

Slowly, and now less laboriously, they skirted the northern shore, came to the low-lying barren with its growth of Labrador tea shrubs and stunted tamaracks, through a tangle of water-lilies and duck-grass, that impeded their progress, passed a tiny island, black with tall spruce and hemlock, came to and turned up the sluggish brook that zigzagged through the heart of the barrens. Chris saw that the brook was much lower than on that early spring evening when he had accompanied Noel on an inspection of his traps. Vegetation had progressed wonderfully. Everything was green, and on the bushes, nameless to him as well as to Bob, at that time, bloomed the purple flowers of the swamp honeysuckle. On little mud flats, left by the receding freshet, they saw snipe, and once a wood duck with a frightened quack rose and flew eastward. Back in the deep woods beyond the barren a partridge drummed.

The mosquitoes were annoying. And now a new pest of the Canadian woods, the black-fly—a tiny insect not unlike the more civilised house fly, but savage, drawing blood at every bite—introduced himself to the adventurers. Bob lighted his pipe and kept them away from his face at least, but his wrists and the backs of his hands suffered. Chris was entirely at their mercy. He tied his handkerchief about his neck, and between paddle strokes made excited slaps at his face and head.

And yet so enchanting was the scenery, that neither had any thought of turning until they had gone to the end of navigation. Birds sang in the alder thickets, blue dragon-flies chased each other through the air over the water, darted along the edge of the barren, disappeared to reappear a moment later. In the soft mud were the deep tracks where some huge animal had wallowed and, crossing the brook climbed out, for the green bushes were spattered with mud and trampled down.

"Perhaps a deer," whispered Chris, turning his face to Bob.

Rounding a bend, they saw bunches of green roots floating on the surface of the water, and along the shore more tracks.

Suddenly Chris stopped and in a tense whisper begged Bob to cease paddling. His quick ear had caught the sound, far ahead, as though someone were dipping water from the brook and pouring it back from a considerable height.

They strained their ears; again came that strange sound, and slowly died away. With one accord they dipped their paddles, and as silently as was possible for two novices, sent the punt around the next bend, beyond which the brook ran quite straight for about fifty yards.

"Whatever is it?" whispered Chris, adding, "I thought it would be here."

Bob shook his head. "It's around the next bend," he whispered back. "I hear it now."

The banks had grown higher, were flanked now with thick clumps of alders, and here and there a tamarack, gaunt and dead, reared its straggly limbs skyward.

Once Chris thought he heard a low champing sound like that which a horse makes feeding. But he said nothing. A few yards more, at the most, and—

As he drove his paddle down into the soft mud to stay the boat's progress, he was conscious that Bob had done likewise, but his eyes were glued on that odd-looking monster but a few yards ahead, and his blood hammered madly in his veins.

He could see the great black hindquarters, the long legs of an animal as big as a horse. But where was its head, if head it had? Then he remembered Noel's account of how moose feed. Of course: the head was under water. He could now see the neck, the coarse mane as it moved from right to left searching for juicy roots at the bottom of the stream. And then there was a sudden upheaval of water, a pair of black ears appeared, then the long head and ugly face of an enormous cow moose, the water pouring from it in muddy streams. She flipped her ears, gave her head a mighty shake and stood, her great jaws working as she chewed those succulent roots.

Chris felt himself trembling with excitement. He glanced around at Bob, received his brother's whispered admonition to make no noise and turned again to the interesting scene before him. Suddenly he saw the animal's flanks stiffen, her ears go back, the great nostrils quivering as she drew in deep breaths. Then, slowly, she turned her ungainly head and looked at them.

So near they were they could see the long lashes flickering over her small black eyes. Then the hair on her neck stood up. Bob dipped his paddle, backed water swiftly, for there was no knowing what the animal might do. But she had no intention of following them. Slowly she swung her head about, walked methodically to shore, drew her huge bulk up on the bank, stood a moment calmly surveying them, then glided into the alders. For a long time they could hear her breaking brush as she made towards the green timber at the foot of the ridge.

Chris gave a deep sigh, turned to Bob. "How jolly," he said, "we've seen our first moose, Bob!"

And they turned the boat and paddled towards home.

CHAPTER 8

BROOK FISHING

The morning of the 24th dawned fair. There was not a cloud in the sky. The sun shone on green pastures, on meadows and hillsides that already showed tender shoots of grain and hay. For in this northern climate Nature, when once she sets about the task, works overtime to produce her harvest.

The immigrants were astounded when, day after day, the sun shone with never an hour of mist. Often rain fell during the night as though there were some working arrangement between Aquarius and Saturn[14] for man's especial benefit.

Chris awakened at daybreak, got up, dressed, made the fire in the kitchen stove, and, having called Bob, got his milking pail and went out. He glanced over to the Clowes homestead, noted with satisfaction that smoke was coming from their kitchen, and, whistling merrily, went down to the milking yard. He was glad the teacher and Bob were going with them to the Keswick.

Mrs. Alison had packed the lunch the previous evening in one of Bob's army knapsacks.[15] Minced eggs there were, a plentiful supply of ham sandwiches, buttered slices of bread, doughnuts, and cookies. Sid had promised to take a frying-pan and a piece of pork, and they were going to fry trout fresh-caught from the stream. He had also promised to provide a "boiling kittle",

---

14 Aquarius, the Water Bearer, is a large but faint constellation in the Southern sky [https://www.space.com]. Saturn, the Roman god of agriculture, was associated with the sun [Wikipedia].

15 Bob had presumably served in World War I.

the which Chris was now Canadianised enough to know was nothing more or less than a tin kettle which campers use in boiling water for tea making.

They met the Clowes party at the highway end of the lane. Winnie and Miss Allen were attired in garments appropriate to the occasion. The former had on a pair of Sid's knickerbockers and an old canvas shooting jacket, the teacher blue overalls and a sweater.[16,f] And during the day she was the occasional butt of Sid's humour. He insisted on addressing her as "Mr." Allen.

Before entering the woods all stopped for the purpose of "doping up"or "anointing" as Sid termed the rubbing on of fly oil to drive off mosquitoes and black-flies. He had prepared five small bottles of the mixture, which he informed the party contained olive oil, tar, and pennyroyal. He gave a bottle to each, and, following his example, they generously applied it to the hands, the back of the neck, and face.

"Now," said Sid, "we're ready for the beggars." And swinging his pack over his shoulders, he took the lead down the tote road or portage, as the winding road through the woods was called. Bob came next, then Miss Allen, Winnie, and Chris last. Times there were when, the wheel tracks not being too deep, the teacher and Bob walked side by side; but for the most part the party went in Indian file, following the well-worn centre trail made by the feet of lumbermen on their way to the logging camps.

Occasionally Sid stopped to draw the attention of those behind him to the track of a moose or deer—once the small imprint of a fox's feet that had been made after the last rain. Indeed, as Sid swung along ahead, he continued to throw

---

16   Before the 1930s women couldn't buy ready-made women's trousers. But it was impossible to walk through the underbrush of the Canadian woods in long skirts; so they borrowed men's clothes.

out bits of information that were highly instructive to the immigrants. Once he paused and glanced at the sun on his right. "If you're ever out here and get lost," he warned his hearers, "you want to remember that the lake lies east and west. So, if it's in the morning, travel a little to the right of the sun, if it's the afternoon, to the left. In any case you'll strike the lake and can easily get around the lower end and hit the tote road. Of course, if the sun ain't shinin' you can climb a tree and see the clearin's on the ridge. The ridge is as high as any of the mountains—as high as Lawrence Peak. Then make straight through the woods. You'll come out all right," he added, with quiet confidence.

Winnie Clowes, turning her brown eyes on Chris, said: "To hear Sid talk you'd think it was all as simple as taking a drink of water. It's not. I was turned round myself once down in that bit of woods in our back pasture." She paused, then added, with a smile, "I was most scared silly."

Chris smiled back at her. This confession from the girl more than half cancelled her rudeness to him on previous occasions. "A pretty good sport after all," he mentally conceded.

The tote road now wound round the base of a ridge covered with mighty birch, maple, and beech, with fir, hemlock, spruce, and a smaller growth of mountain laurel bearing cup-shaped purple flowers; wild raspberry bushes, alders, moose wood, and here and there a white birch. Said Sid: "In the fall the deer come from the swamps and feed on the raspberry bushes, and when there's a good crop of beech nuts they feed on them till the snow gets too deep." Waving a hand to his left, he added: "I've seen the side of the ridge there all pawed up after a snowstorm." He suddenly stepped off the side of the road, drew their attention to a small maple, the bark a couple of feet from the ground entirely scraped off, on two sides. "That's where a buck stopped to rub the velvet off his horns last fall," he explained. "It was down there," he added in a matter-of-fact voice, "where

I got my first deer, four points to a side. Father and me had to swamp a road[17] part of the way, to get him out."

He stepped back into the trail again and walked on, the others following slowly. It had been a stiff climb the last half-mile, but now the ground sloped abruptly. Far off on their right the forest stretched in an unbroken line for many miles. "There," said the informing Sid, "lays the valley of the Keswick. That's good moose country."

Now, on either side of the tote road, for a hundred yards, raspberry bushes grew as high as one's head. Beyond was green timber, spruce, fir, cedar, and hemlock. Here and there great logs, thrown to the ground by half a century of storms, lay rotting, moss-covered. Farther on they passed through a strip that had been cut by the lumbermen the preceding winter. Score upon score of stumps stood where once proud hemlock and spruce had reared their tops towards the sunlight. Little paths, down which the logs had been twitched,[18] led off the tote road into the woods.

To Chris, every step he took held something of interest. Once when the tote road led through a piece of low land with alders on either side, a hen partridge, with a brood of young ones, rose from almost beneath their feet. For a moment he glimpsed half a dozen small shapes scurrying wildly for shelter; then they were gone. Sid had stopped. "They're just the colour of the undergrowth," he said. "Like as not you're looking right at 'em and can't see 'em."

Hardly had he spoken when the mother partridge flew into the road ahead. She lay over on one side, her wings outspread, dragging her body along one of the tracks made by the tote wagons.

---

17   To make a road through a forest by felling trees and bushing out undergrowth [OED].

18   Pulled. Horses "twitched" logs through the winter woods to tote roads.

"Oh," cried Miss Allen, "the poor thing's hurt. What a shame!"

Sid broke into a loud laugh. "Yes," he cried mockingly, "poor thing. Poor little motherless baby partridges."

The mother hen was still dragging her body ahead of them, every moment or so making an effort as though she were trying to fly. Sid broke into a run, got within a few feet of her and then, wonder of wonders, the apparently wounded bird rose, and, straight as an arrow, flew off through the trees.

Sid turned his brown eyes on Miss Allen, simulating deep sadness. "Poor old wounded mamma partridge," he said, and pulling his handkerchief from his pocket made believe he was wiping tears from his eyes.

Miss Allen picked up a dry branch from the tote road and flung it at him. "Outrageous boy!" she cried. "Stop making fun of me and explain why the bird did that—I mean why she dragged herself along ahead of us as if she were hurt?"

Sid took out his bottle of fly oil and, while he methodically anointed his face and neck, said: "Some folks say animals and birds haven't got reasonin' powers. But I say they have. For why? Well, just because that mother partridge wanted to get us away from her brood, she made believe she was hurt, knowin' we'd follow her. See'd 'em do it a hundred times. Better put on some more dope," he added, "the flies are gettin' bad."

They put on the "dope" and walked on, single file, along the green aisle of the forest, that led unbroken, as Noel Polchis had told Chris, thirty miles to Nashwaak Lake, and on to the salmon waters of the Miramichi.

Coming to a fork in the road, Sid stopped and, pointing to that leading off to the left, said: "That goes over Lawrence Peak way and Fish Lake.[g] This on the right to the Keswick. If ever you're over here alone you want to remember that." He turned to the teacher. "Want a five-minute rest, Mr. Allen?" he asked.

She laughed and said yes, so they all sat down and rested until Sid, with a flourish, drew out his watch and said, "Time's up."

A half-mile farther on he stopped. "Hark!" he said.

They listened. A strange sound, that might be running water or a wind springing up, fell on their ears. "It's the Keswick," explained Sid with shining eyes, and bounded ahead, the others gaily following. The trail now sloped abruptly downward, was strewn with small pebbles washed out in the spring by melting snow and rain coursing down the slopes on both sides, which were covered with alders, small birch, and maples. And ever that murmuring sound became more definite; unmistakably a brook purling over a rocky bottom.

Fifty yards more and, the trees suddenly thinning, they could see water sparkling in the sunshine, here and there a foam-flecked pool. A few more yards and they had reached the brookside, had laid down their packs on the log bridge. On either side of the stream the timber, at some remote period, had been cut, leaving a cleared space of three or four rods[19] in depth, and stretching for about a hundred yards down-stream. Here the grass was quite high, and blue with violets. Said Sid: "We'd better have a bite of lunch before we begin fishing. If anyone wants tea I'll boil the kittle. If not, we'll wait till we've got some trout, then boil it at noon. What do you say? There's a spring handy where I can get some drinkin' water."

All immediately protested that a lunch, with spring water, was sufficient for the present. Each was eager to try his luck on the stream. So the packs were opened and, after Sid had brought a kettle of water, they sat down on the bridge and ate sandwiches and drank of Sid's Elixir of Life, as he termed the spring water.

Sid and Chris finished first. "Come on, old boy," said Sid, "and we'll cut some poles," and led the way to a clump of alders. Sid picked out the straightest and slenderest, cut off the desired

---

19 A rod is about 5 metres.

length, and handed them to Chris to top off the branches. When they had five prepared they went down to the bridge, and Sid attached the hooks and lines. Then he drew from his pocket some split shot,[20] laid the line in the groove and, disdaining the aid of a rock, used his teeth (despite Miss Allen's horrified warning) to press the edges firmly together.

"Oh, what's the difference, Mr. Allen?" mocked Sid. "Besides if I break a tooth I can get a gold one," he added, a twinkle in his brown eyes; "I've always wanted one."

"What a boy!" exclaimed Miss Allen, laughing into his whimsical face, "why do you want a gold tooth? They're horrid things."

Sid grinned, and, disdaining a reply, opened his bait can, picked out a wriggling worm and dexterously threaded it on the hook. "Now, Mr. Allen," he said, "take this and see if you can catch a trout. If you don't you shan't have any for dinner."

Winnie Clowes refused Chris's aid and baited her own hook. "I'm not afraid of angle worms or—even snakes," she said.

"Now, I'll tell you," said Sid, when all were properly outfitted, "some of us should go upstream and some down. How about you Winnie—you've been here before—taking Bob and Mr. Allen up-stream, and I'll guide Chris? We'll go down a mile or so and be back by two o'clock anyway. You can take your party as far as the falls and fish down."

This was agreed to. Amid gay farewells and Sid's admonition to "Mr. Allen" not to get her overalls wet, the up-stream party departed along the trail which skirted the brook to the falls.

"Now, old chap," said Sid, "we can begin. If you want to you can fish from the bank; I'm for wading. But," he made a slap at a mosquito that had alighted on the back of his hand, "we'd better put some dope on first."

---

20 A type of lead shot where each pellet is cut part way through the diameter; it used to be used as a line weight in angling [Wikipedia].

Chris followed Sid's example and waded the brook. At first the water made his feet and legs tingle, but he soon got used to it, nor minded it more than Sid.

And now he was treated to a sample of trout fishing such as his imagination had never pictured possible. From beneath the bridge Sid suddenly whisked a ten-inch trout. It went far over his head and landed in the grass. Chris, who was on the opposite side, splashed across and joined Sid who, having picked up the trout, was about to deposit it, still wriggling, in the capacious depth of his pocket.

"Please, Sid, let me see it," said Chris.

Sid flashed him an odd look. "See it?" he asked. "Oh, we'll get lots of them,"

However, he passed the trout to Chris, who took it in his hand. "Isn't it beautiful! What wonderful colouring. See, Sid, those carmine spots along its sides."

Sid grunted. "Oh yes," said he, "I suppose it's pretty, but it will taste better than it looks."

"I doubt that," returned Chris. Then looking at Sid added: "You'll tap it on the head before putting it in your pocket, won't you? You see," he went on, "it isn't right to make them suffer any longer than necessary."

"Oh," said Sid, giving him a sharp look, "I see. Yes, I suppose you're right. But tap it on the head! There's an easier way than that, old boy."

He took the fish, slipped a brown forefinger into its mouth and bent the head back. "You break their necks that way," said Sid calmly. "Now, you try down there where I got this. Don't let the bait lay on the bottom; let it float along the side of the bottom log and when you feel a nibble give a quick jerk. You'll soon catch on."

Chris did his bidding. He let the bait float down the length of the line, then, as he had seen Sid do, began to draw it gently towards him. Suddenly he felt a tug; the slim alder bent, and he pulled, pulled with both hands and, with a mighty heave, threw pole, line, and fish far from him up the bank.

Sid was shouting: "You got a whale! A whale, I tell you! Oh, crickety, it's a pounder, sure; as big as any I've seen caught here." He held the prize up to Chris's excited gaze; and, as Chris clambered up beside him, added: "We'll tap this chap over the head," took out his knife and with a few sharp blows put the thing out of pain. Then he laid it down on the grass. "He is a beauty," he said, paused, and went on a trifle bashfully. "I never thought much about them before to-day—I mean how pretty they are. A trout was just a trout; a whole lot better to eat than a chub or a sucker, that was all."

"Yes," said Chris, "it's the same way with sunsets or a landscape. With some they're just trees or a bit of red or purple cloud. A—a sort of accident of nature. But to me they're wonderful."

Said Sid: "You're an odd fish, so you are. But I see what you mean." He bent, cut off some bunches of grass with his knife and wrapped it about the trout and placed it beneath one of the packs.

As they splashed through the shallows Chris's heart was singing little tunes of joy. It was wonderful to be following this wayward, laughing brook. At every bend was something new, here a wild cherry in bloom, there a white dogwood; up the hillside a laurel flaunting its cup-shaped purple flowers. And on the banks were violets—white and blue and yellow— and massed plots of fragile blood-root. And now and then, the shallows washing its green, the wild mint. He thought of those days of toil following the plough and harrow, the hours on his knees in the garden. It was all worth while when one had the privilege of indulging in an outing like this.

The trout were plentiful and hungry, and soon the forked alder, which Sid had cut for him to string his catch, was heavy with the speckled beauties. Sid's pockets were bulging with them. So expert was he, so sensitive to every nibble, that he had twice as many as Chris. But Chris felt no pang of jealousy. Indeed, often he left the brook to gaze on some strange flower along the bank.

Once Sid grasped his arm and pointed ahead of them. "I saw a deer's head down there by that leanin' birch," he whispered. "Just be quiet. He'll step out in a second. Look! There's his neck—a buck! See his horns; they're in the velvet yet. See, there's his forequarters. Oh, what a shot!"

Chris felt himself trembling with excitement. He saw the buck step gingerly into the centre of the stream, lower its head and drink. Then it turned its head, saw them, gave vent to a shrill snort, and bounding across the brook, leaped the bank and disappeared. Another deer followed and yet another, their long necks outstretched, their white flags erect. With magnificent leaps they reached the bank, sprang up the wooded slope and vanished. And for some moments naught was heard but a succession of snorts, growing ever fainter.

"Crickety!" cried Sid. "If it'd been the hunting season we could have downed 'em all!"

"Yes," murmured Chris, but without enthusiasm. He might shoot the buck in season but not the doe or fawn. Besides, the day was too delightfully charming to entertain thoughts of slaughter.

He was surprised to find that Sid was not well acquainted with the different birds. Sid, of course, knew the "Canada" bird, that tiny, white-throated sparrow, whose liquid notes proclaiming "Sweet! Sweet! Canada! Canada! Canada!" fell on their ears with haunting sweetness. He knew the different kinds of owls and the kingfisher, blackbird, blue jay, and a few others. But the thrush family, the chewink, the warblers, were mere names, and he couldn't tell one from the other. Regarding the names of the wild flowers, too, he was, save for a few of the commoner ones, like the violet, blood-root and adder's tongue, obliged to admit his ignorance. The linnae, hepatica, anemone, arbutus, trillium, were all just "May flowers".

Chris was disappointed not to know all about them and decided when he got home to send to St. John or Montreal for a book describing and picturing in colours the wild-flowers of Canada, as well as a book on birds. He didn't know until some time later, that Miss Allen, had he accompanied her up-stream, would have been able to satisfy his thirst for knowledge.

But what Sid lacked in knowledge of bird-life and wild-flowers, he made up for by being deeply versed in wood craft and animal life. He knew the names and habits of most of the fur-bearing animals, the different methods of trapping them as well as the value of their pelts. He knew the different trees, the uses for which each was best suited, their commercial value in the log and when sawed into lumber. And, too, he amazed Chris by his uncanny sense of direction. Once he said: "Chris, if you wanted to get back to the bridge, and there wasn't the brook to follow, which direction would you go?"

Chris, without hesitation, confidently turned and pointed up-stream, but towards the right.

Sid smiled, shook his head and said: "You're wrong, old boy. It's over to the left," and pointed straight at the sun.

"But," began Chris, "the brook couldn't have made such a half-circle. It—"

The brown eyes of Sid were twinkling. "Come," he said. "I'll show you. We've enough trout." And leaving the stream he struck off through the woods. Chris, every fibre of his being dumbly protesting that Sid was going in the wrong direction—that they would both be lost—followed. Not for worlds would he show his companion that he was in a funk. He noted that when Sid came to a fallen log or thicket of small growth, he made a detour, then swung in line again with the sun. They jumped innumerable rabbits, and routed a porcupine, which Sid chased with a stick until it sought refuge up a tree. Once, at the edge of an alder swamp, a red fox stood and calmly regarded them a moment, then slunk off and was lost to sight in the dense growth.

They had travelled, it seemed to Chris, a half-mile when, straight ahead, a little to the right of the sun, his ear caught the sound of water. So sure was he that Sid had taken the wrong direction, he was prepared to see, not the Keswick, but another stream. But a moment later they entered a small clearing, and there, a few rods distant, was the bridge with their packs reposing where they had left them.

Said Chris: "Sid, you're a perfect wonder."

Sid modestly disclaimed the tribute. "The others aren't back yet," he said. Then, "Oh it was nothing. I knew if I bore slightly to the right of the sun, we'd reach the bridge. Still," he advised, "I wouldn't try it alone, if I were you; not until you get more acquainted with the lay of the land."

"But," asked Chris, "could you have made it without the aid of the sun?"

"Oh yes; sure I could," said Sid; "but it wouldn't be so easy. But I'd have struck the ridge there on our left and followed along its base. Of course," he confessed, "I don't boast of being a woodsman like Dad, or Noel Polchis; and I suppose in a new country I'd get lost quick enough; but if there was running water I'd follow it and in time I'd get out."

Chris gazed admiringly at his friend. "If I were half as good a woodsman as you, Sid, I'd be quite happy," he said, and followed Sid to the brookside.

"Now," said Sid, taking out his knife, "let's clean our fish," and proceeded to take his catch from his pockets.

A merry half-hour followed, and when the trout had all been cleaned, washed off, and wrapped in wild cabbage leaves, they gathered dry sticks from the edge of the forest and started a fire on some dry shingle beside the brook.

Said Sid: "Plenty of people—fishermen and hunters—make their fires handy to the woods, instead of in the middle of a tote road (takin' care to find a damp, earthy place) or along a brook, like we are. And then they go away without puttin' it out; a wind springs up and carries sparks into the dry woods. And thousands and thousands of dollars worth of timber goes up in smoke. When we're through with this fire I'll dash water on it; make sure not a spark is left. Because if a fire did start here, the warden could arrest us. And we'd either be put in prison or fined." He ceased, went to a clump of alders, cut a forked stick a couple of feet in length, came back and forced it into the sand beside the fire. Then he cut another, longer; sharpened one end, thrust it into the soft earth of the bank and allowed the other end to rest in and beyond the forked upright. "Now, for some water," he said, and picked up the smoke-blackened boiling kettle. And as he climbed the bank, a chorus of shouts from the bridge above reached their ears. Chris glanced up, and there were Bob, Miss Allen, and Winnie, each holding up to his gaze a string of trout.

For many a day Chris was to remember this hour. The trout were cooked to a crispy brown, in pork fat, by Winnie, who assured everyone that she could do them much better than Sid. Bob saw to the making of the tea, and Miss Allen spread a cloth she had brought on the grass, and laid out the sandwiches, doughnuts, and other eatables. And then, when all was ready, they sat in a circle, and, between laughter and jest, ate the repast which Sid said was fit for a duchess. Bob had placed himself beside Miss Allen, whether intentionally or by accident Chris didn't know, though he did notice that Bob, who was usually so quiet and shy in the presence of the fair sex, had cast off his reserve, and once, instead of addressing her as Miss Allen, called her Ellen. "Pretty good for old Bob!" thought the boy.

And meanwhile, birds sang in the thickets, crickets chirped in the grass, and the brook ran its melodious course over the shallows, and in the blue heavens the sun sank ever farther westward. A great peace filled the lad's heart, and, when the dishes were all washed and repacked—and some crumbs scattered about for the birds—and they filed along through the forest homeward, Chris felt that never in all his fourteen years of life had he had such a glorious day.

CHAPTER 9

INNOCENT INTRUDERS

The middle of June came, and in the meadows the wild strawberries had ripened. Day after day, during that week, Bob and Chris, and sometimes Mrs. Alison, sat in the grass—now a couple of feet high—and filled their kettles with the tiny fruit. It was arduous work, for the sun was boiling hot, and it took so many berries to fill one's dish. And often Chris glanced down at the lake and longed to go swimming, or take the boat and paddle out to the spring hole by the pine stump and try for a big trout. On the lake there was always a gentle breeze, while here in the field, hidden by the grass, it was close and hot. But the gathering of wild strawberries, as the boy knew after the first day, was worth while. A saucer of them, covered with cream and sugared, was the most wonderful treat he had ever put down his eager young throat. They had a flavour of their own. And the smell of them.... "They were more than a mere accident of nature," Bob declared. It was as though in her wonderful laboratory Nature had brought to her aid all the alchemy of the ages to produce the wild strawberry. And every day, as they brought in their heaped-up dishes, Mrs. Alison put them in the stewing kettle and covered them with sugar, and in the morning she put them on the stove to make into jam, and when they were sealed in jars they were stored in the cellar for the winter days.

One day a car came over the ridge, stopped on the side of the highway near the meadow, and the occupants, five in number, got out, carrying tin cups and pails, climbed over the fence and began picking in the Alison meadow. Chris was indignant. "What right have they to come into our field?" he said to Bob.

"They can see, must know, the farm is now inhabited." He was for going over and warning the intruders off the place, but Bob asked him please not to. "A party came Monday and picked in Clowes' field," he added.

"But they have no right," argued Chris.

Bob smiled. "Possibly not, but I believe it's done in this country," he said.

Chris refused to be mollified. "How would they like it if I went to their home and took a pail and walked into the pasture and milked one of their cows? I'd be arrested. They'd say I was taking what didn't belong to me."

Bob smiled again, started to reply, but Chris went on:

"Besides, they're tramping down our hay."

"So are we," returned Bob.

"Oh yes," admitted Chris, "but that's different. It's ours."

He remained silent a few moments, unable to further explain himself, but within him was a deep resentment at this intrusion of outsiders on his father's domain.

"You see, old boy," said Bob, "although this thing wouldn't be tolerated in England, it *is*, here. And being in Rome we've got to do as the Romans do. These people, now, would doubtless be surprised if they were told they were trespassing, they would think us pigs. Possibly, if they reason at all about the matter, it's to the effect that there are plenty of berries and we can't possibly pick them all. But I fancy they haven't given it a thought. It's done in this country."

Though he said nothing in reply, Chris was still inclined to be belligerent. He picked in silence, filled his tin cup, emptied it into his pail, and after a while found himself within a few feet of a shock-headed,[21] fat-faced youth about his own age.

"Hello. Fine day," said the stranger. "Berries are plentiful, ain't they?"

---

21 With a thick, untidy mass of hair.

For a moment Chris glared at him. Then the youth smiled, a smile that went far towards disarming Chris of his anger.

"There's lots more than last year," went on the smiling youth. "But the year before, this field was red with 'em. Say," he held up to Chris's gaze a stem containing a cluster of unusually large berries, "ain't they beauties?" he asked.

Chris nodded. "You come here every year?" he demanded.

"Oh yes," was the calm reply. "We always figger on makin' at least one trip in the berryin' season. Make it a sort of picnic; bring cake and sandwiches and a freezer of ice-cream." He paused. "I say," he went on, "when we have our feed, you and that other chap—is he your brother?—well, you and him come on over to our car and we'll give you the feed of your life. It's not store ice-cream, but made by ourselves. And Ma flavoured it with maple syrup and put butternuts—" He paused, quite out of breath, then added: "If there's anything I like as well as ice-cream, it's bananas. Do you like bananas?"

Chris couldn't repress a smile. He gazed into the fat, good-natured face of the trespasser (as he still stubbornly called him in his heart), then answered:

"Yes, I like bananas, but I haven't had one since I left England, three months ago."

"Oh, Holy Moses!" ejaculated the youth, his blue eyes bulging in amazement, "three months without a banana! Say, is that possible? You ain't stringin' me?"

Chris shook his head, at which the youth set down his cup in the grass, jumped up, and without a word started at a run across the field towards the car. Chris gazed after him in astonishment. What an extraordinary boy, he thought, and began picking berries again.

Soon he heard someone running, panting, and looking up beheld the fat youth beside him, a banana held in each hand. He flopped beside Chris, held out the bananas. "Quick," he said, "take 'em, eat 'em. Oh, Holy Moses! Three months! Three months!" he added in an awed voice.

"Thank you," said Chris, and took one of the bananas from the outstretched hand. "You have the other," he said.

The boy shook his head. "Not me," he protested. "Take it, quick. Put 'em down you. Do you know," he added, "I could eat a bunch of bananas, a whole bunch. Some day I'm going south, where they grow, and I'm going to buy a bunch. They say you can do it for twenty-five cents—and I'm goin' to lay on my back and—just eat bananas." He tossed the remaining banana in Chris's lap as though he were anxious to rid himself of a temptation that might prove too strong for his banana-loving nature and, picking up his cup, set resolutely to work again.

Chris finished one of the bananas and took the remaining one to Bob, and coming back, sat down beside his new acquaintance. How jolly glad he was that he hadn't followed his first impulse and ordered this boy and his people from the field. Yes, there were enough berries for all, and the grass—it would soon right itself.

For the next hour he kept company with the fat boy, learned that his name was Charlie Patterson, and that he lived about three miles the other side of Millville, on Maple ridge.[h] "We ain't far from the river," said Charlie. "Ever been there?"

Chris shook his head.

"It's some river, the St. John, I can tell you. It starts away up in northern Maine and then flows through New Brunswick till it reaches the Bay of Fundy. My dad's an old rafter. He takes rafts of cut lumber and logs down the river to Fredericton for anyone that wants him to. It's some job, I can tell you. Last summer I went with him a trip. It was a lumber raft. There was a big long sweep[22] at one end for steerin'. But sometimes, when the current carried us close to shore, that wasn't enough, and Dad and Joel Perkins had to get their long sweeps out and work mighty hard to keep us from groundin'."

---

22 A long steering oar.

Chris was intensely interested. "How jolly," he said. "You must have had a glorious time."

"Yes," nodded Charlie, and went on with his recital. "We made a fire on the raft in a little tin stove—you can fold it up when not in use—that Joel brought, and cooked potatoes and boiled cod fish. It was pretty nice, I tell you. And when night came, we tied up to an island and camped under a big tree. Next morning I found a stone tomahawk, used by the Indians a couple of hundred years ago. It hadn't any handle, but there was a notch around the middle of the axe where they tied the thong to hold the handle."

As he talked, reciting the bare facts of the capture of a New England boy, John Gyles, and his years of life among the Melicetes of the St. John, Chris's imagination was carried backward over the years. He pictured this New Brunswick land when it was peopled by the Melicetes, who, finally allied to the French adventurers by treaty and religion, and in many cases by marriage ties, fought the encroachments of the English for more than a hundred years.

Sitting here in the grass, Chris let his gaze wander to the lake and the ridges beyond. He thought of his friend Noel Polchis (present chief of the Melicetes on the reservation below Woodstock), and it was hard to believe that the soft-spoken Noel was a descendant of those very warriors whose loyalty to the French lasted until the gallant Wolfe won victory and death on the plains beyond Quebec. He remembered how Noel, in speaking of trapping and hunting moose and deer, had said: "My fader come here to Taffy Lake; an' his fader; an' his fader. And so they come, long before white man come up the big river. And they shoot the moose with bow and arrow, an' tan him hide an' make moccasin an' snowshoe an' clo'es."

For a few moments the lad let his imagination flit backward over the years when these smiling fields were nothing but forest, and the Indians held sway over the vast domain, living their own lives unconscious that across the sea other men lived, fought, and lusted for wealth and power, and one day were to come, conquer, and take all. Little wonder, thought the boy, if at times, brooding on their past glory, the Indians protested at the white man's law which decrees that: "You may take a fish and a deer and a moose, and you may trap at such and such a season, but break the law and you shall suffer." So engrossed was the boy with his thoughts that his companion spoke twice before he heard. He looked up.

"We're going to have the big feed now," said Charlie. "Come on; we'll get your brother and soon we'll introduce ourselves to that freezer of ice-cream."

CHAPTER 10

ADVENTURES IN FRIENDSHIP

Hardly was the strawberry season over—giving them short respite in which to hill the potatoes anew and sprinkle them with Paris green[23] to kill the bugs—than the raspberries were ripe. They grew along the line fences,[24] about the stone piles—those mute monuments to long hours of back-breaking labour by the former dwellers on the farm; and out the tote road a mile, where lumbermen had denuded a half-acre of standing timber, the bushes were thick, the fruit abundant.

And as the days passed and the jam making and preserving went on, the shelf in the cellar fairly groaned with its burden. Spiced gooseberries there were, and gooseberry jam, and red currants and rhubarb, the latter found growing in the garden when they came.

And now the hay was ripe for cutting, and all day long, from morning until night, was heard the busy sound of mowing machines. Long since, Mr. Alison and Bob had gone over the machine they had purchased with the farm. It was rusted—had lain for three years in an ill-boarded outhouse, exposed to the snow and rain. Some parts were missing, but these were replaced from Millville. Every bolt was oiled, grease lavished upon the axles, the scythe sharpened.

They all worked—Mr. Alison, Bob, and Chris. In the afternoon the hay was raked into windrows and piled in cocks

---

23 Copper acetoarsenite, a highly toxic emerald-green powder that used to be used as an insecticide [Wikipedia].

24 Fences that run along the boundary lines of a farm.

against possible rain and the heavy night dews. In the early mornings they went forth again, spread the hay out for the sun to dry further; and at length Bob harnessed the horses to the big hay rack, and while he stood on the ground, and with his fork lifted the hay up into the wagon, Chris and his father "made" the load. Then into the barn between the mows the great cart was drawn, and the unloading began. By the end of the week it was filled almost to the eaves. Then, for a time, there was again respite from labour, save for an occasional Paris-greening of the potatoes and the usual barn work. They had purchased another milch cow,[25] and now Mrs. Alison was able to exchange fresh butter as well as eggs with the man who made weekly trips over the ridge in a covered cart filled with an odd assortment of groceries and dry goods. Days there were when Bob and Chris, accompanied by Sid Clowes, got into the boat and paddled about the lake, fished in the spring hole, from which they pulled many a fat trout, and made occasional voyages past the island and far up the thoroughfare to where a maze of fallen and standing dead logs (called by Sid "rampikes") made, at this height of midsummer water, progress into Kilburn Lake[26,i] impossible. Here, one day, they pulled up the boat and, guided by Sid, walked along the shore to Kilburn Lake. It was a hot afternoon—the temperature around eighty-seven or ninety— such an afternoon as drives the forest creatures to seek cooling streams and lakes.

Emerging from the woods on the edge of a small bay, the adventurers suddenly came on a great bull moose, half up to his middle in the muddy water, feeding on weeds and lily roots. Hastily they crouched behind some small spruce bushes and watched him. He stood, head on, and went about his

---

25 A cow kept for milking.

26 Kilburn is the middle lake in the 3-lake chain collectively and incorrectly named Taffy Lake on modern maps.

afternoon lunch unconscious of their presence. Down would go his pendulous nose, lower and lower, until his eyes, ears, and great antlers had disappeared, till only the big flanks remained visible. For an incredibly long time—it seemed at least a couple of minutes—the beast was thus submerged, its flanks moving now to the right, now to the left, as he searched the depths for his food. At length, with a mighty commotion, he stood up, the water pouring from his sides, from the enormous palms of his antlers, from the long tuft of hair on his neck below his muzzle (Sid called it the "bell"). He worked his great jaws rapidly, impatiently flipped his long ears at some disturbing fly. Chris noted that the upper third of one ear was quite white.

Whispered Sid, his eyes sparkling with excitement: "That's the big bull old Tom Lindsay called out one night last fall at North-East Lake.[j] Must be. Can't possibly be two bulls in these parts with one white ear. Gee! Look at that spread of horns; fifty-five or sixty inches, anyway, with the pans as broad as mother's ironin' board. They're in the velvet now, covered with a coat of fur, but when the middle of September comes he'll have it all rubbed off and be in fine fightin' trim. There, he's going to put his head down again. Oh, what a shot!"

For a quarter of an hour more they sat as still as statues, watching the monarch of the forest feeding, then, without disturbing him, they crept back along the path to their boat.

All the way down the thoroughfare and lake, until they landed and tied the boat, Sid talked of the moose.

"That's the one Tom Lindsay called out and shot at, sure as sin," he reiterated. "He said the tip of one ear was white, probably'd been injured either in a fight or by a bullet, or else just a freak of nature. Anyway, he fired every shot in his magazine at him, and the animal never flinched; just moved off lazy-like, across the barren." Sid paused a moment, then resumed. "Tom was disgusted, thought he must be losin' his shootin' sight. But when he got home he tried out his gun and found that the foresight was away to the left. And then he remembered how just before he'd got in his boat to go up the deadwater,[27,k] he went to pick up his rifle where he'd stood it against a tree, and it'd slipped and fell to the ground. The sight must a hit a small rock," added Sid. He paused again as though to allow the tragedy of the affair properly to sink into his hearers' consciousness, then went on: "Tom said he come on Old White Ear after the first snow. He was standin' on the side of a ridge, feedin' on a moose-wood tree,[28] when Tom come along. Tom says the bull's shoulder was behind a big birch, so he just moved a few feet to get a better sight of him. And as he did so he stepped on a stick. Crack! As the bull sprang away and raced up the ridge Tom fired twice. But he says he didn't hit him. At any rate he followed the tracks over the ridge and down into a cedar swamp and away over beyond Spruce Peak[29] to North-East deadwater.[l] Perhaps," sighed Sid, "Tom will get Old White Ear this fall. If Tom can't get him I don't know who can—unless—" he paused—"it would be Noel Polchis. Outside of Noel, Tom's the best moose caller in these parts."

"But," said Bob, "is it good sport to get a moose that way? Isn't it rather taking a mean advantage of the bull?"

Sid emitted a snort of disgust. "A mean advantage!" he echoed. "Not by a long shot. Oh, well," he conceded, "it might be on a young bull, but not on a wise old chap like White Ear. The man that can call *him* within shootin' distance has got to be a whole lot better than expert. You got to call so fine that a cow can't even tell the difference. You see," added Sid,

---

27 A stretch of watercourse with no perceptible flow. Deadwater is a distinctively New Brunswick term.

28 Acer pensylvanicum, or striped maple, a small North American species of maple [Wikipedia].

29 This could be either Big Spruce Peak or Little Spruce Peak; they stand side by side. See the Geographical Addendum at the end of this book.

"every hunter in the woods is hootin' away on a birch-bark horn. And you don't fool even a young bull much more than once. As for it being poor sport—well—is it to be compared to breedin' a lot of birds like you do in England, and then sittin' on a bench an' shootin' 'em? I've read about how they do it, and I call it tame. Of course, though, it's all the way you feel about it."

Both Bob and Chris liked Sid immensely. They conceded that in many ways he was uncouth, that he had a large vocabulary of swear words which, when he was excited, he seldom failed to use, and that he murdered the English language horribly. But apart from these failings he was a splendid companion, was possessed of a fund of dry humour, generous to a fault, resourceful, and quite fearless in the face of danger, and, as they found later, as loyal in his friendships as he was bitter towards those he considered his enemies.

Sid had read few books. In fact, other than a semi-weekly newspaper printed in the city of Fredericton forty miles away, little that was interesting to a boy of Sid's age found its way into the Clowes' homestead. One evening he came over to Allison's and found Chris reading an old copy of the *Boy's Own Annual* that had belonged to Bob.

Chris immediately put down his book. Sid sat down, talked of the weather, the state of the crops, as though he were thirty, instead of fifteen years of age. Then after a moment's silence, he said:

"What were you reading, Chris? What sort of a book is that?"

"It's the *Boy's Own*," answered Chris. "I was reading 'The Smugglers' Beacon'."[30]

"'The Smugglers' Beacon'?" echoed Sid. "It sounds good. I've read a few things about trapping, but not many stories." He paused, gazed dreamily over the hills.

---

30 *The Boy's Own Annual* was a year's issues of *The Boy's Own Paper* bound into a book and sold at Christmas. "The Smugglers' Beacon", by Henry Frith, was in the 1892-1893 volume, which GFC read when he was nine years old.

"Oh," cried Chris. "You've never read *The Last of the Mohicans,* or *Deerslayer?*"[31]

Sid shook his head. "But," with sudden interest, "I'd like the *Deerslayer*, anything about hunting."

"It's not so much about hunting," explained Chris. "It's about a man whose name was Nathaniel Bumppo; but he was such a good shot they called him 'Deerslayer'. And he had a gun he called Killdeer. He was a great foe of the Iroquois Indians, and he and Chingachgook—the 'Big Serpent'—fought on the side of the English against the French and their allies the Iroquois. There's five books all written about the Deerslayer and Chingachgook. And oh, Sid, you've surely read *Treasure Island* and *Kidnapped?*"[32]

Again Sid shook his head, a mournful shake that went to Chris's heart. Eagerly he said: "I've got all these books, Sid, and I'll lend them to you. First the *Deerslayer*, because I think you'll like it better than *Kidnapped* or *Treasure Island*; not because it's a better story, but on account of your loving the woods and the hunting so much."

"Of course," nodded Sid. Then added: "Would—would you mind reading me a little of that smuggler story now?"

Chris glowed with pleasure. "Why, of course not," he said, and picking up the old book, published away back in the eighteen-eighties, opened it on his knees, found the first chapter of "The Smugglers' Beacon" and began.

He read until the sun went down behind Petong Mountain, until the last rays of the afterglow had faded from the lake, and dusk settled over the fields, and it was impossible to see the print. And all the while he had been conscious that the boy at his side was drinking in every word, was, in fact, carried away with the story, for, at times, he murmured some excited

---

31   Adventure novels by James Fenimore Cooper.

32   Adventure novels by Robert Louis Stevenson.

comment, and more than once growled out a curse on Mr. Jasper Murdock, the sinful old uncle of the hero of the tale. Now he heaved a deep sigh and said: "Could you please read me a little more by lamplight, Chris?"

It was more than a polite request. It was the appeal of the awakened soul of a youth realising for the first time the witchery of a well-told tale of adventure. And with gladness in his heart, Chris told him to come in and they'd light the lamp. Of course he'd be happy to read more. He felt that in doing so he'd be repaying Sid somewhat of the debt he owed him for the knowledge of woodcraft and angling, the tales of hunting, which this friend had so unselfishly imparted to him.

It was ten o'clock when, with a sigh, Sid rose and declared he *must* get home. They had left the hero in the clutches of the pirate John Paul Jones on board the *Bonhomme Richard,* beating up the English Channel towards the coast of Scotland. As Chris rose to accompany Sid to the door, he said: "Come over tomorrow night, Sid, and we'll finish it; that is, if you like."

"If I'd like," repeated Sid, his face beaming. "Just as soon as the cows are milked I'll be over; sure thing. And thanks. And thanks for the *Deerslayer,* Chris."

As Chris went to his bed that night he was happier than he had been for many a long day. He had opened up a new world—a world unknown, undreamt of, by his friend.

CHAPTER 11

DUCK SHOOTING

It was the first day of September and the season for shooting ducks was now on. Chris Alison, a warm sweater beneath his jacket, sat on the back-door step, his eyes now roving over the bosom of the lake, now turned impatiently across the road to Clowes' lane. He wished that Bob and Sid would hurry. But of course—yes, the teacher had returned to take up her duties in the schoolhouse on the ridge, and Bob would want a few minutes' conversation with her. But Bob had said he'd only be gone ten minutes! The boy again looked at his watch. Already twenty minutes had slowly fled and no sign of Bob or Sid. True, Miss Allen had been away six weeks, and six weeks was a long time. Two more weeks and the season for big game would open, and, by the end of September, perhaps a few days earlier, Noel Polchis would be wending his way over the ridge to Taffa Lake. Could it be possible that it was actually only four months since Noel Polchis had stood beside him down there by the grain field and said his good-bye? It seemed ages ago. Then they were but sowing the grain; now it was cut, safely stowed in the barns awaiting the coming of the threshers, who even now were making their way over the ridge, stopping at those farmsteads whose owners didn't own threshing machines, taking as pay a toll—one bushel of grain for every ten threshed. In a week, or ten days, potato digging would begin. Already the tops were quite brown.

The boy glanced at the sun—near the western horizon. How short the days were getting. And the evenings and nights were quite cool. Only this morning there had been a light frost on the after-grass[33] in the meadows. Down by the line fence a maple flaunted faintly crimson leaves. The blackbirds had already wended their way southward, and soon, so Sid had informed him, the robins would also go.

The boy could hear his mother's voice inside singing an Old World song, as she knitted at a stocking for her husband. How brave she was. Never had he heard her complain or voice a wish that she was back in England. "This is my home," she had said so many times. But he knew, oh so well, that she often longed to see and set her foot on English soil. As for himself, he was quite contented. As his father and Bob had so often declared, this new country was a land of immense possibilities. One had only to work honestly and intelligently and the future was assured. And the forest! His eyes strayed to the vast wilderness of trees across the lake—what a playground! It was not owned by one individual, but was everyone's heritage. No keepers to say: "You shall not fish or shoot here." No signboards warning off trespassers. How wonderful!

So engrossed was he with his thoughts that he didn't see Bob and Sid approaching, and he gave a little start when suddenly Sid's voice fell on his ear: "Come on, old scout," was his friend's greeting.

Chris rose, glanced at Bob's face, noted that his brother's eyes were sparkling, his cheeks beneath the tan flushed. Then the boy picked up the knapsack containing the cartridges from the doorstep, seized the paddles, and, Bob having got his gun, they proceeded down towards the lake.

Sid carried a long muzzle-loading shot-gun.[34] "It ain't quite up-to-date," he had remarked, in speaking of the gun to Chris, "but it's capable of great execution."

---

33 Grass that grows after the hay has been cut.

34 An older type of shotgun, in which the shot and and propellant charge are loaded from the forward, open end of the gun's barrel [Wikipedia].

They reached the lake, untied the boat and got in, Sid taking the stern paddle, Bob the bow paddle. Chris sat on the centre seat.

They paddled diagonally across the lake to the thoroughfare, turned in at the brook and proceeded up this for a couple of hundred yards where, beside a small juniper tree on the edge of the barren, Bob got out.

Said Sid: "You can crouch under the tree and you'll have a good view of any ducks coming either up or down." As he swung the boat out into the stream again he added: "We'll stay till dark anyway."

Chris now had Bob's paddle. As he swung his arms in rhythm to Sid's stroke, his eager eyes swept the shore for signs of moose tracks. Only once, since that day when, in company with Sid and Bob, he had seen the big bull in the little bay up Kilburn Lake, had he got a glimpse of old White Ear, as Sid called him. Perhaps even now he was making his way through the woods to this very brook to feed on lily roots; or (banish the thought) he had left the vicinity entirely, was away over Trout Lake way or to the Guimac waters. As he knew from Sid, moose often change their feeding ground, and especially after the first frosts, roam over vast distances.

There were no mosquitoes or black-flies now. They had either migrated elsewhere or, as Chris hoped, had lived their lives and died. Pesky things! The air was filled with forest odours. Here and there along the edge of the barren the boy glimpsed the pitcher plant faintly touched with red. Off across the barren, where the frost had touched the young maples, shades of pink relieved the monotony of the dark spruces and hemlocks.

Sid swung the boat towards the shore near a clump of alders. "We'll pull up here," he said. Chris got out, and Sid, picking up his gun, followed, and with much puffing and grunting, they dragged the boat out of the water until it rested on a cushion of low, spicy-smelling bushes which Sid reminded Chris were

Labrador tea. "Steep 'em," added Sid, "and they don't make too bad a drink. Leastwise I've heard the natives of Labrador use it instead of tea."

Chris picked one of the long, spear-shaped leaves, turned it over and found that the under surface was covered with a soft, rust-coloured wool.

"Come," said Sid, "get placed, here, beside me. Here's an old log we can sit on. That's right." He put a cap on the nipple of his antiquated shot-gun. "You keep your eyes peeled for birds coming from up the lake and I'll cover the territory west of us. Of course they may not come here to feed until after dark, but—Jee-rusalem! there's Bob's gun now. Wow! both barrels."

"Look—look," cried Chris, "there's two—coming right up the brook—flying low."

"Here, take the gun," commanded Sid. "When they get opposite, fire—a little ahead. Yes, do," as Chris demurred, and he thrust the gun into his chum's protesting hands. "Quick, let 'em have it."

Chris was trembling. He lifted the long, heavy fowling-piece and, as the two ducks went hurtling by, fired, as Sid had suggested, slightly ahead of the foremost.

As he tumbled backwards, his shoulder numbed by the kick of the gun, Sid grasped the barrel from his hands and began reloading. "You got one," he cried. "He fell over there by the alders. Hurt?" he asked, pouring a charge of shot down the muzzle. "I had a pretty good load in."

Chris rose and picked up the ramrod, which had fallen. "No," he said. "Not much. It was glorious." He watched Sid tear a piece of paper from his pocket, thrust it in the muzzle of the gun, send it home with the brass-shod ramrod. Feverishly Sid placed a new cap on the nipple, and as half a dozen black shapes sped out of the now fast darkening sky, stood, his dark eyes gleaming, feet braced apart and the stock of the old muzzle-loader resting against the muscles of his right arm.

Bang! went Bob's breech-loader.[35] Bang! again. The boys saw one of the flock of five ducks go hurtling downward and saw the remainder swerve sharply to the left and disappear over the black line of forest towards Kilburn Lake.

Back among the timber along the edge of the barren an owl sent out its lonely, "whoo-whoo!" Came a night hawk soaring majestically along the shore opposite; a splash as of a fish leaping.

"Look," said Sid, "it's a mink."

From the distant ridge shrilled, what seemed to Chris, the cry of a human being, lost. He turned startled eyes to Sid. "A wild cat," was Sid's comment. As he spoke, up went his gun; his eyes squinted for a brief fraction of a second along the barrel, then followed the report.

"Two," he chortled. "Come on, Chris, get the boat in. We can't see to shoot any more to-night, so we'll pick up what we've got."

They pushed the boat over the crackling shrubs into the stream, and seizing the paddles, jumped in.

"Let me manage it," said Sid. "You stand ready to lift 'em aboard. There—there's one. Good," as Chris reached out and flung the duck into the bottom of the punt. "There's another. Got him? Leave him for me. My, what a beauty! Now for the other. Yes, right ahead, old boy. There he is, right close to shore. Lean over; don't fall in. The water ain't so deep, but there's three feet of soft mud. Good. Hurrah! Now for picking up old Bob's bag."

They paddled swiftly down the brook. Bob, who had heard them coming, was standing up, a dark shape against a darker background. His clear voice came over the water:

"What luck?"

---

35 A firearm in which ammunition is loaded via the rear (breech) end of its barrel [Wikipedia].

"Three," the boys called out in unison.

"I fancy I got four," said Bob. "Easy; there's one by the leaning tamarack. Two more are down this way below me, and the other fell in the grass. I'm afraid it's so dark we shan't be able to find it."

But they did, all three landing and hunting for some time among the grass and bushes, close to the edge of a little backwater. Then they trooped merrily back to the boat.

The stars were reflecting their glory in the lake when they entered it, and a new moon hung, a sickle of gold, above the tree tops lining the southern shore. From the pasture came the tankle, tankle of a cowbell, the bleat of a sheep, and, from the depths of those black shadows on the northern shore—vanguards of a countless host of maple and spruce and hemlock—the sharp bark of a fox.

They moved across the waveless lake, only the sound of Bob's paddle against the gunwale and the wash of the water against the bow to break the silence. The wild, weird beauty of the scene impressed even Sid. He paddled with short, noiseless strokes, steering straight for the narrow landing.

When they reached the shore and clambered out, Chris felt cold and cramped. He took his load, a couple of the ducks tied together by their legs with a piece of cord, swung them about his neck and, paddle in hand, followed Sid up the path to the field above. The grass was wet with dew and soon his feet were wet, but the exercise of walking soon sent the warm blood racing through his veins, and he was happy, gloriously happy. He had bagged his first duck.

Chapter 12

Harvest-home

The coming of the threshers was, as Chris learned, an epoch in the lives of the people on the ridge. Everyone seemed prodigiously excited, for, until they had come and gone, the yield of grain per acre was an unknown quantity. One could make a guess, of course, but it was considerably more satisfactory to *know*, to a bushel, what the ground had produced.

They finished at Stebbins', moved on to Hopkins' farm, set up their machine, and from morning until night could be heard the tut-tut-tut of the gasoline engine. Then Mrs. Alison began baking bread and pies and cakes. The thresher and his men had to be "put up" for such time as they were engaged. And three men besides her own, working all day in the open, were sure to require a great deal of food. Where they were to sleep was at first a problem, but by the time they were moved down from Hopkins', matters were straightened out. Bob and Chris were to "bunk" together, leaving the latter's bed for two of the men, and Mrs. Clowes kindly offered to put up the third man. Here was yet another evidence of that kindly spirit which animates those residing in rural Canadian districts. Mr. Alison was keenly appreciative. As he said to the family one day during the breakfast hour:

"It's so much nicer for new settlers to purchase farms close to Canadian farmers rather than cling together and form new settlements."

Bob nodded and Mr. Alison went on: "Of course it would be vastly pleasing to have at least a few friends of the homeland. I should like it immensely. But what we have lost in one respect we have gained in another. By watching the methods and taking the kindly advice of our Canadian neighbours we have been so much more successful, made fewer mistakes than had we joined a community of all English settlers." He paused a moment, helped himself to another slice of toast, then went on. "We should have made innumerable mistakes and without doubt have been positively disheartened. If I were an official of the Immigration Department in England, my suggestion to prospective immigrants would be to settle close to the people of the country to which they intended emigrating, to mix with them freely, make notes of their methods and accept advice in the spirit in which it is given. If such counsel were given, there'd be fewer disgruntled settlers writing back home of their failures."

All heartily agreed with him.

On Wednesday, the 15th of September, the threshers drove into the yard, set up their machinery, got the gasoline engine going and began threshing the oats.

For a time Chris "tended" half-bushel. That is, as soon as the half-bushel measure was full to the brim, he quickly pulled it to one side, replaced it with an empty, then emptied the first into a two-bushel bag. At first he thought it splendid fun. It was so interesting watching the oats pouring from the chute into the measure, keeping the tally and seeing the filled bags grow rapidly in number. But after a couple of hours his interest waned, and he asked Bob—who was clearing away the threshed straw from the mouth of the machine—to exchange jobs.

Bob smiled, said: "All right, kid, have a try at it by all means. But it isn't as easy as it looks."

Chris took the fork and soon found that he had made a bad bargain. As quickly as he worked, he was not quick enough to keep the straw away from the immediate area of the threshing machine. His shoulders, arms, and chest ached; the sweat poured into his eyes and the straw dust half-choked him. But he worked courageously and stubbornly on, would doubtless have dropped at his task before giving in, had not Bob kindly relieved him. Then was Chris contented to go back and tend half-bushel again. As the sacks rapidly filled and he heard one of the men say that the yield was better than at Hopkins' and almost equal to Stebbins', his pride in the farm increased: "Pretty good for newcomers," he told himself.

At twelve o'clock sharp everyone ceased work, trooped to the wash bench beside the kitchen door, removed some of the dust and dirt from face and hands, went in and sat down to the table in the big room.

There was little conversation during the meal. They ate heartily and quietly, and when done pushed back their chairs and lighted their pipes. When the pipes were empty they strolled out-doors and, as Chris had seen so many men in this country do, took from their pockets a plug of tobacco, and bit off a chew. Indeed, when not eating or smoking, it seemed to Chris that they were chewing tobacco. However, it did not seem to hurt them. They were big, healthy-looking chaps, bronzed with the sun and wind and rather jolly; chock full of quaint anecdotes and experiences of the woods and river driving. It seemed that every second man he had met in the last six months had either worked in the lumber woods or done stream-driving in the spring; often both.

These men spoke of operations to be begun over Lawrence Peak way, during the coming winter. Handly, from Millville, was even now over there building shanties. He hoped to get out a couple of million feet of logs, according to one of the men.

Two million feet of logs! The figures staggered Chris's imagination. Could it be possible? And then he heard them go on and recount how, before the mills were built at Tobique and Edmundston and Van Buren, as many as one hundred millions of feet of spruce, hemlock, and fir had been floated down the St. John to the booms at Fredericton. What a country!

How great its resources! His pride in it was daily growing. More and more, he reverenced the hardy pioneers who had first come to this land, made homes for themselves in the wilderness, built towns and cities, linked the east to the west with railroads; who, when the call of their race sounded, went in their hundreds of thousands overseas and fought and bled and died to preserve Anglo-Saxon ideals. Yes, as Bob repeated over and over again, the Canadian farmer was resourceful, familiar with, not one kind of work, but many; the axe was his favourite tool. Put one of these men in the woods with an axe and some matches and he would perform wonders: build a cabin, clear land, fashion a boat from a pine, construct deadfalls to trap wild animals, build bridges. As Bob half-jokingly remarked: "An axe, on a green shield with a wreath of Eddy's matches, should be the pioneer's coat-of-arms."

The result of that first day's threshing was one hundred and fifty bushels of oats. On the morrow would be more, since no time would be lost in moving and setting up the machines.

In the evening, when the supper dishes had been cleared away, a fire was built in the big fire-place, and the men sat round and smoked and talked of the price of grain, hay, potatoes; of the lumbering industry, the price of pulpwood, hardwood, spruce logs; of hunting deer and moose. How Stebbins had shot a buck in his oat field that very morning, and, armed only with a partridge-gun, had met a bull moose face to face on the portage across the lake.

When nine o'clock came the pipes were put away and each man sought his rest. To Chris this had been a wonderful day, and he could understand now how the coming of the threshers was looked forward to by the people on the ridge.

The following morning, as he tended half-bushel, he saw Sid, a gun over his shoulder, striking across the field towards the upper end of the lake. An envious feeling possessed him. He wanted to stop work, get Bob's gun and hasten after his friend. In spite of his ever-growing interest in the threshing, the big woods called him. In fancy he could see the little trails, the sun filtering through the trees; partridge, startled at his tread, racing among the undergrowth, or, with a rush of wings flying along the forest aisles. Alas, there was work to be done! One couldn't always play. When the threshing was done and the potatoes and roots gathered in and stored, he could indulge his fancy. Now he must have patience.

About eleven o'clock came to his ears from the distant ridge, three shots, fired in rapid succession. "That's Sid's gun," he told himself, and hoped his friend had had luck. The minutes passed, but he heard no more shots, but just as he was about to go to dinner, he saw Sid emerge from the woods and hasten across the field. Sid's hat was in his hand, his coat was off, and, as Chris ran to meet him, he noticed an exultant look on the flushed face of his friend.

With a few bounds Chris was by his side. Before his lips could frame the question: "What luck?" Sid said, his voice quivering with excitement: "I got a fine buck,[36] old chap, a sixpointer—fat as butter. I bled him and now I'm going after Father. We'll have to take the horse to get him out."

"Splendid!" cried Chris. "Oh, Sid, you're a wonderful hunter." He glanced at his friend's face admiringly; then, a tiny note of pathos in his voice, added: "I do wish I'd been with you."

Sid flashed him a queer look. "So do I, Chris," he said. "I'd have asked you to go, but of course I knew you were tied up threshin'. I'll be in the same box next week when they come to our place." As he walked along by Chris's side, he recounted the morning's hunt, how he had routed the deer in the low land and stalked him up and to the very top of the ridge, where he came on him feeding on some ground hemlock. The first shot was a

---

36   Sid and Chris think of shooting game as sport, but in this period
     frontier farmers depended upon shooting moose and deer for
     food for the winter.

clear miss, the second a hit in the neck, the third, fair behind the shoulder. "I'll bring you over some meat this afternoon," concluded Sid, as he branched off towards his own home.

Chris thanked him and walked slowly in to his dinner. And he would have given worlds to be able to quit work that afternoon and accompany Sid and his father over the ridge to where the buck lay.

That evening, true to his word, Sid came over and presented Mrs. Alison with a hind-quarter of deer venison, and, because she knew Sid had a particular liking for her make of pies, she bade him wait, and bringing out half of a blueberry pie, set it before him. Sid murmured his thanks and fell to; and when he had quite finished said, his blue eyes fixed admiringly on Mrs. Allison's: "You make the best pies of anyone on the ridge, so you do."

The yield of wheat was not up to expectations, but this was put down to the fact that the ground had not been fertilised for three years, rather than to any fault of the seed. With proper fertilisation, and fall sowing, there seemed no reason that, given good growing weather, both the oat and the wheat crop would be much more satisfactory another year.

On the fourth day, the threshers moved over to Clowes', and the Alisons began potato digging. This was done by a horse-drawn digger—a machine that Chris had never before seen in operation. For a week he followed the digger, picking up the potatoes and depositing them in a basket which, when filled, he emptied into barrels placed at intervals along the rows. It was uninteresting work and hard; his back ached and often he had to take off his shoes to get rid of the fine gravel that somehow managed to find its way in and bruise his feet. When night came he was so tired that he could hardly put forth enough energy to help with the milking. Sleep came readily, but two nights in succession he dreamed over the day's work. As he said to Bob, it was bad enough to pick potatoes during the day, but to pick them all night also was going it a bit strong. However, when the last row had been picked and the barrels safely in the cellar, he was again conscious of a feeling of pride and satisfaction.

Since the duck hunt, he had not had a gun in his hands. No time for duck or deer or moose hunting; but now he would have a day or two to himself before turnip pulling. He had been thinking several times lately of Noel Polchis, wondered whether the Indian would remember his promise. Every morning now there was frost on the ground; the moon was nearly at the full and according to Sid and others he had talked with, it was the very best time for calling moose.

Several hunters had gone over to the Keswick deadwater. All had managed to secure deer, but, save for one party—one of the members of which had called out a moose but couldn't get him within shooting distance—no one in the last ten days had seen a bull with a head large enough to pass the law. As Sid had explained, a bull must have at least three points to a side. To shoot one with less was to incur a heavy fine. The game warden had been coming and going with unexpected frequency. Twice he had turned back hunters who had failed to purchase the necessary licence to hunt moose and deer. And he had been warning all whom he met against leaving camp fires burning. The season was very dry, the fall rains late in coming, and over in Maine as well as in Quebec province, forest fires were reported to be raging.

Chapter 13

Noel Polchis Again

As Chingachgook kept his promise to the Deerslayer, so did Noel Polchis keep his promise to Chris Alison. Chris was just coming out of the barn from milking, when he saw Noel before him, heard the Indian's "*Illigiskit.*" Chris set down the pail of milk and springing forward, grasped the Indian's hand, "Yes, yes, *Illigiskit,* such a splendid day, Noel."

Noel smiled. "Good," he said; "you learn talk Injun quick. You no forget. How you fader and mudder an' Bob?"

"All well," cried Chris. "All quite well, thank you. And how about *your* family, Noel?"

"Dey well, Chris," answered Noel, "what you tink? When I go home last spring I find 'nodder baby. Good job I get plenty musquash. I buy'm cow."

Chris smiled, "But when did you come, Noel? There's no morning train from Woodstock. You didn't come—"

"Last night," said Noel softly, "I go by here in dark; pitch'um tent down on point. And what you tink? Dis morning 'bout tree o'clock I hear bull moose grunt 'way up on bog; grunt two time; old bull. Me know. He grunt down deep in him throat, young bull make short sound like year-old pig."

"Oh, Noel," said Chris. "Of course you haven't heard yet, but Sid got a deer last week over on the hardwood ridge. He gave us a quarter. I never ate venison steak before."

"Deer steak good," commented Noel. "Moose steak better I tink." He paused a moment, his brown eyes on the boy's eager young face. He added: "I get up daybreak, go get canoe. I pitch'm to-day. How you like it go up deadwater with Noel 'bout five o'clock? We try for moose."

"Oh, Noel," cried Chris, "I'd simply love it, and—" he paused, hardly knowing how Noel would take the request he was about to make. He stumbled on: "Noel could you—could we take Bob and—and Sid Clowes with us? Sid has been such a good friend—has taken me fishing over at Keswick, has taught me so much about the woods. I'd hate to have any enjoyment that Sid didn't share. You...you understand, Noel?" He ceased and gazed hopefully up at Noel's impassive face.

For several moments Noel said nothing. It seemed to the boy that his friend was debating in his mind whether he would or would not allow any other than himself to accompany him. He broke the silence by saying: "Of course, I know it's awful cheek for me to ask you, Noel. But you know how it is. Bob's my brother and he never heard a moose called, and Sid Clowes—Oh, Noel, you see how it is—Sid's been such a jolly friend."

"I see," said Noel solemnly. "Noel—what you call him—understands. Sid your friend; you want your friend to have some good time. All right, I take Bob an' Sid too. I take Bob anyway. I take Sid because he your friend."

"Oh, thank you, Noel, thanks a thousand times! Come, Noel, you haven't had breakfast; come to the house and have some with me."

Sudden shyness swept over the Indian. "I boil the kettle 'fore I come up," he said; "I go back pitch'm canoe. Him leak in bow."

"Oh, but do come," pleaded Chris. "Mother is frying bacon and pancakes—buckwheat pancakes, Noel—"

He thought he sensed a slight weakening in the Indian's manner and followed up his advantage. "Come along, Noel," he urged, "and then I'll go down with you while you pitch your canoe."

Said Noel: "I no go in house. I stay on doorstep."

"Oh, no—no you don't. I couldn't allow that," said Chris. "You'll sit between me and Bob at our table." He picked up his milk pail, linked his other arm through Noel's, and despite the Indian's protesting voice, urged him along beside him.

At the door he was met by his mother. Proudly he began. "Mother, this is my friend, Noel Polchis. I'm bringing him in to have some of your pancakes."

Mrs. Alison smiled, shifted the pancake flipper from her right to her left hand and shook hands with Noel. "I'm so glad Chris brought you…" she hesitated, then added that which did more than an hour of conversation to make him feel at ease. She spoke his name: "Noel."

Chris put his milk pail on the kitchen table, and led Noel into the other room, where his father and Bob were sitting. Bob sprang up and greeted Noel cordially. Then Chris unfolded the programme for the evening. "It will be wonderful," he added excitedly. "Noel's the best moose-caller in the country. And just think," he appealed to both, "Noel heard a bull grunt early this morning. Might have been Old White Ear—"

During the half-hour that followed, Chris was not altogether happy, for the reason that he realised that Noel, in spite of their efforts to make him feel at ease, was nervous. He ate heartily, but said little, merely giving "yes" or "no" to the questions put to him, kept his eyes on his plate and, when he had finished—which he did before any of the others—pushed back his chair and rose.

"I go out on doorstep. Smoke 'm pipe," he said to Chris, and, picking up his hat from the floor by his chair went, but not before Mr. Alison had jumped up, and taking a cigar from the mantel, pressed it into Noel's hand.

A little later Chris joined him, and side by side they walked across the frost-encrusted meadow and through the woods to Noel's camping place.

Chapter 14

The Moose-call

At five o'clock that afternoon, Chris, with Bob and Sid—the latter carrying his father's magazine rifle,[37] a broad belt filled with cartridges, and a long hunting knife, and looking as he was, a very Nimrod—stood at the boat landing, awaiting the coming of Noel Polchis. All were dressed for the occasion, in wool garments, with an extra short coat or mackinaw, to put on when they should reach their destination. For the nights were extremely cold for October. Sid had informed them that there had been a skim of ice on the pond beside their house that very morning when he led the horses down to drink.

The sun was far down in the west, leaving the lower part of the lake half in shadow, and all that mass of colour was reflected on the glassy surface. He sighed. Oh, but this little world was beautiful! He loved it all. Suddenly he saw Noel paddling up the lake, with each stroke of his powerful arms lifting the bow of the canoe several inches out of the water. And as he came he left a long V-shaped wave of crimson behind him.

Chris waved his hand. He saw Noel's paddle flash in the sun in answer. "Good old Noel," he thought, "how jolly of him to take Sid too."

Noel swung his craft in shore, brought it to a quivering standstill within a few inches of the beach. He said: "You, Bob,

---

37 A rifle capable of repeated discharges from a single barrel between ammunition reloads. This is typically achieved by having multiple cartridges stored in a magazine and fed into the chamber by the bolt [Wikipedia].

you heavy, you get back here, and you, Sid boy, you get in bow. Wait, I get out; hold canoe."

He got out, bent and steadied the frail craft while he directed the embarkation. Gone was his shy reserve of the early morning. He was at home in his great outdoors.

When all were seated to his liking he stepped in, sank easily to his knees in the stern and pushed off. The canoe, loaded to within four inches of the gunwale, was now much steadier and yet it seemed, to Chris, incredible that such a frail thing could carry them safely across the lake.

Noel swung his paddle noiselessly, and in a few minutes they were skirting the shores of the thoroughfare. Arriving at the mouth of the brook, Noel went more slowly, examining the water and shores with great care. The sun had now gone down, leaving a chill in the air, and the barren, with its growth of shrubs, stunted cat-spruce, and an occasional blighted tamarack, looked more than ever cold and forbidding. Beyond, the black line of spruce, cedar, and firs, stretching back to the foot of the ridge, seemed to Chris too compact to allow passage for a large creature like a bull moose.

There was no wind; not a sound save the faint dip of Noel's paddle. Once Chris heard a light splash ahead and saw the tail of some water animal as it disappeared beneath the surface. Noel whispered the one word: "Musquash."

Where the brook narrowed and the alders began, Noel swung his canoe to the left-hand shore. Then in a low voice he spoke: "You, Bob, you, Sid, get out on bank, stay under that tree," he pointed to a white birch. "I take Chris an' go back hundred and fifty yard. Then I call. Maybe moose come over there," he pointed opposite, "maybe he come to Chris and me. If he come to you, shoot'm." He pointed to the moon that had swung up over Taffa Lake. "By'm-by, when it get darker, moon light up barren, make light as day."

He reached out, caught hold of a Labrador tea shrub and steadied the canoe until Sid had got safely to shore, then he added a few words of advice in case a moose did come to the call. "When you shoot, shoot straight, and don't shoot Chris an' me. Break some branches off little spruce and sit down." He ended, and allowed the canoe to float out from the shore. Then he swung the nose down-stream and paddled steadily until he was opposite the spot where, a month earlier, Sid and Chris had drawn the punt up on the shore and shot the flock of ducks. Here Noel ceased paddling and laid his paddle carefully in the bottom of the canoe. Chris half turned to watch him. He saw Noel draw from beneath the stern a cone-shaped horn of birch bark, saw him rise to his feet and slowly turn until he faced diagonally across the barren towards that black mass of evergreen trees and the ridges beyond.

In his intense interest the boy forgot that he was woefully cold. His teeth ceased chattering; he sat spellbound, gazing at his friend. He saw Noel raise his arm, put the small end of the horn to his lips, then, as the moose-call fell on his ear, wild, weird, unlike any sound of man or beast that he had ever heard, a strange thrill passed over him.

"e-e-e-E—U-u-u-u—R-r-r-r-r-r!"

First two short calls, then a third, longer, the notes rising gradually until they filled the air, went shivering across the barren, penetrated to the fastnesses beyond, to sink finally to a low, plaintive ending, alluring, and, to the boy, inexpressibly sad. He could hardly believe that the man in the stern of the canoe had made that sound. Noel stood, his hand holding the horn now at his side, his bright eyes on the distant line of forest, head slightly to one side, lips partly open, as his ear sifted the silence for an answer to his call.

A few minutes he stood thus, then he turned, sank to his knees in the bottom of the canoe and picked up his paddle. There was no sound as he dipped it, but the canoe began to move swiftly and silently, only a little purling at the bow as it parted the water.

A few yards farther on, by the leaning tamarack, Noel stopped, brought the stern close to the right-hand shore, stepped out and, grasping the gunwale amidships, steadied the craft until Chris was safely beside him, then, catching hold of the middle thwart with both sinewy hands, he lifted the canoe bodily from the water and deposited it on the barren. Next he cut with his knife a little pile of green boughs from a young spruce, placed them beneath the tamarack and bade Chris sit down.

Night had now fallen, but the light from the moon shone slantwise over the barren, so that any large animal approaching across it to the brook would be easily seen.

Suddenly, from the foot of the lake, a loon sent out its ghostly laugh. Then all was silent.

Noel stood on the boy's right, his rifle against the tree trunk, the birch-bark horn in his hand. For perhaps five minutes he stood thus, nor uttered a word, then he raised the horn again to his lips.

Chris watched him, fascinated. As the call rose to the highest pitch he saw the horn slowly describing a circular motion, once, twice, three times, and at the end of the third, Noel had bent his body, shoulders, and head, until, at the final notes, the large end of the horn was only a few inches from the barren.

As at the previous call, so now did a nameless thrill pass over the boy. There was in it something wild, primeval, and, though it was all so new to him, he felt in his heart that the call was true, the notes perfect, that he was listening to a master of the art.

"e-e-e-E—U-u-u-u—R-r-r-r-r-r!"

He watched Noel carefully lay the horn down, then rise to his full height and again stand with that air of strained attention, as of one listening for some sound afar off.

Suddenly, on the silence, from the depths of that dark mass of trees at the foot of the ridge, came a sound, a tremendous crash, as of a tree falling to earth. He saw a grim smile linger for a second about the Indian's thin lips, then Noel whispered, "He come," and, rifle in hand, sat himself down beside the boy.

Five minutes passed, ten, not another sound. The silence was intense, oppressive. The moon sailed higher. By its light the boy could see little sparkles of frost on the leaves of the Labrador shrubs. His feet, and his back between his shoulders, were uncomfortably cold. He had a vision of the snug living-room at home, a warm fire, a book. That crash over there across the barren couldn't have been a moose after all. He glanced at Noel; saw that his Indian friend was still intently listening. He looked, thought the boy, like a bronze image, so silent he was. An involuntary shiver passed over the boy. Without a word Noel reached behind him, picked up his mackinaw, and placed it about the boy's shoulders.

Hardly had he done so than Chris heard another sound, not so loud as the first, like the sudden snapping of a dried limb of a tree—not directly across the barren, but farther west; saw the Indian rise, his horn and gun in hand, and move soundlessly to the margin of the brook, a few yards distant.

He watched intently Noel's motions, expecting and hoping to hear him call again. But no. He saw Noel crouching by the very edge of the stream, saw him dip the horn in the water, slowly raise it, and from the height of a couple of feet let the water pour back into the stream.

For a moment there was again silence, then from up the brook came a hoarse grunt that sent the boy's hair on end and his heart beating wildly against his ribs. He turned his eyes in the direction of that sound. Again it came, piercing the frosty night, "Ough! Ough!" And then, in the light of the moon, he saw a great black shape burst from the rim of trees, move swiftly across the barren towards the brook where Bob and Sid were waiting. As it swung more into the open, he could see the great flanks rising and falling with clock-like precision, the enormous head upflung, the wide antlers arched majestically over the high shoulders. Oh, it was wonderful—wonderful! Gone the cramped, chilled feeling from his limbs, thoughts of the warm fire at home. He wouldn't have missed all this for worlds.

For a brief second he withdrew his eyes from that great animal racing with express-like speed across the barren, and sought Noel; with difficulty made out his friend's form crouched below the encircling shrubs. Would Noel call again? he wondered. He heard the animal splash through some water, emit another grunt, then he saw him, standing sharply outlined against the alders, a hundred yards away, and only separated from Bob and Sid by a narrow brook. Would they never shoot? He saw the moose slowly turn his head until it was pointing in his own direction. What a head! It must—it surely must be Old White Ear. He saw the lordly creature give his ponderous antlers a shake.

Came a sharp report of a rifle, then another, that echoed over the ridges. He saw the big beast give a sudden leap, go down to his knees, spring up again and come racing along the edge of the barren, then from Noel's rifle shot out a stream of flame, another and another. The boy saw the moose give one wild leap in the air and go down, heard, with a sudden sickening within him, wild thrashing among the shrubbery opposite, that gradually grew still.

The whole thing was like a dream. He saw Noel pick up the canoe, and as the bow hit the water give one mighty shove to the stern and spring in.

A wild hurrah from Bob and Sid. As for Chris, he didn't feel like shouting. The moment was too big, too tragic. Gone was that feeling of elation that had possessed him while the moose was coursing across the barren. The noble creature was over there among the Labrador tea shrubs, dead. Never more would it roam the ridges, seek the cooling waters to quench its thirst and feed on the juicy lily roots. He wished that he was home before the fire reading one of his beloved books.

Then came the reaction; for he was above all a normal, healthy boy. Wild animals, just like domestic animals, were placed on the earth for man's use.[38] For one to say: "I must not kill my cattle or my sheep for it would be taking an unfair advantage of a dumb animal," would be silly. As for a moose, or deer, especially the former, it was a case of the man pitting his skill against animal sagacity. And it required no little skill to call a big bull out of the woods and shoot him. Bob and Sid had done jolly well. As for Noel—who hit the running creature by moonlight—his was a splendid feat of marksmanship.

The boy slapped his arms about his chest and stamped his feet to drive the cold from his body, and watched the movements of Noel Polchis. He saw the Indian return to the stream, launch the canoe and recross. "Come Chris," he said, "get in. We go get Bob and Sid."

Sure enough the bull was Old White Ear. The antlers, according to Noel's and Bob's computing, had fully five feet of a spread, with twenty-six points. As thoroughly as was possible by the moon's light, they dressed the big animal and, leaving it there on the barren, embarked again in the canoe for home. The quarry must be skinned, cut up in quarters and, as Noel said, equally divided among the hunters. "You like him head, Chris?" he asked.

"No—no, I mean, yes," stammered Chris. "But it wouldn't be right for me to take it. If it hadn't been for you we'd never have got it. You called him out, put him down for the count. No, you shall have the head, Noel."

Noel grunted. "I fix antlers on oak shield for you, Chris; make good gun rack," and, as though he considered the matter settled, paddled on in silence.

---

38   This idea has deep roots in Judeo-Christian theology. Its ultimate source is Genesis 1:27-28, where God says to Adam and Eve: "Replenish the earth, and subdue it: and have dominion over the fish of the sea, and over the fowl of the air, and over every living thing that moveth upon the earth."

It was eleven o'clock when, having recounted the night's adventures to his parents, Chris went to his bed and fell immediately into a dreamless slumber.

Chapter 15

An Alarm

On the morning of the 3rd of October a smoky haze covered the country, to the north and north-east. Some of the men of the ridge settlement thought that it might be smoke from the fire in Quebec, others that a fire had started over Fish Lake way. One prophesied that it would soon rain, thank God; that the present drought couldn't continue much longer.

About noon, Richardson, the game warden and fire ranger, came out of the woods, his face and hands blackened, his clothes torn, and physically done up. He stopped at the Alisons', threw his pack from his shoulders, and sinking wearily down on the doorstep called for a drink of water. When it was brought he emptied the dipper at one draught, wiped his mouth with the back of his hand and asked that a horse be harnessed for him at once. He briefly explained that he'd come on a fire early that morning on the side of an old set of camps south of Fish Lake. He surmised that some careless hunters had failed to put out their fire before leaving. Alone, for an hour, he had done his best to fight it; but it had got too great a start and he had left, making the eight miles through the woods in a little less than two hours.

"I'll 'phone the Crown Land Department," he said, "and gather a crew in Millville to go over and fight it." He paused a moment, then added: "We can only do our best; the whole forest is as dry as tinder. And if it doesn't rain…well, with the way the wind is blowing—look out for trouble."

Bob was already on his way to the barn. The warden turned to Mr. Alison.

"I'd like you to get as many men as you can from the ridge to help. Clowes, Patterson, and Hopkins are all good. They can meet me here. I'll be back in less than three hours. You might get your woman to put me up some grub. We'll very likely be over there two or three days; no knowing." He rose, and followed by Mr. Alison and Chris strode towards the stable yard, where Bob was already harnessing the horse to the light carriage. The warden jumped in. "By the way," he said, turning to Chris, "is Noel Polchis still campin' down at the lake?" and at Chris's "Yes, sir,"—"Well, you go get him; we need him. He's the best woodsman in the county. Tell him to meet me at the edge of the woods at three-thirty this afternoon." He picked up the reins, seized the whip and was off.

For a few moments they watched him speeding up the hill leading over the ridge to Millville, then Bob said: "Of course, I'll go and do what I can to help, Father."

"Certainly," said Mr. Alison, and repeated the warden's orders about getting a crew of men from the ridge.

Bob nodded. "I'll put the saddle on the grey," he said, "and rout out as many as I can."

Chris, his heart thumping excitedly against his ribs, touched his father's arm. "May I—go also, Dad?"

"What need?" asked Mr. Alison. "Besides you're to give Polchis the warden's message."

"Oh yes, I know that," said Chris. "I didn't mean I wanted to go with Bob, just now. I meant could I go with the fire fighters?"

Mr. Alison shook his head. "Why, laddie," he said kindly, "you'd be no good over there. You'd only be in danger of your life. No."

Chris's face fell. "But, Dad, he pleaded," I wouldn't be in any danger. I'd be with Noel and Bob. And—Dad, I'm a Canadian now. I'm to live here, and I may as well learn young how to fight fires and things. I'm fifteen now—please, mayn't I?"

Mr. Alison hesitated. He hated to refuse any reasonable request. He wanted his boy to grow up strong and resourceful; but there would be danger. If it didn't rain the fire doubtless would sweep over a vast territory.

"If I were in the Royal Navy," began Chris, "and we met an enemy, I'd have to fight. You'd have me fight, Dad?" His father nodded grimly. "Well, that forest fire is an enemy," went on Chris, "and I don't want to be a slacker. Sid—you'll see—Sid will go."

His father reached out, patted his shoulder. He said abruptly: "You may go, laddie. You're right. I wouldn't have you a slacker," and turned and walked slowly towards the house.

With a shout of joy, Chris flung his cap in the air, deftly caught it, clapped it on his head, and ran as fast as his legs could carry him down the hill towards the point and Noel Polchis.

He found Noel on his knees beside a tiny fire, which he was feeding with alder sticks. Above the fire, on a small platform, were laid slabs of moose meat, which Noel was smoking for future use. He raised his head at Chris's approach, smiled, said, "*Illigiskit,*" and bent again to his task.

Chris gave him the warden's message, adding proudly: "I'm to go too, Noel; isn't it jolly?"

For a few minutes Noel made no remark. He continued breaking the little alder sticks and feeding the fire quite as though Chris had not communicated anything unusual. At length, however, he said: "I smell smoke early this mornin', *Mutjego!* (too bad). John Richardson say I go. I come. John, he smart white man." He said no more, but got his frying-pan, threw in a little fat and some pieces of moose steak, and held it over the blaze. "I have my dinner an' put some grub in pack. We be gone two, three, four day, p'r'aps."

"Oh," said Chris, "it must be awful. You've fought fires before, Noel?"

Noel nodded. "Plenty time," he answered. "One time I fight big fire six day on Sow-back Mountain,[m] nort'-west of here. Sometime not'ing to eat an' drink; squirrel, maybe, or rabbit." He paused to turn over his moose steak. Chris asked:

"But you got it out, Noel, at last?"

The Indian slowly shook his head. "It drive us in lake," he said solemnly. "We stay there t'ree hour; moose come in lake too, and deer. Black bear come in lake too, with cubs; never mind us; come up close. We make raft go 'cross lake. Then wind shift. Good job too; sweep fire back on itself. Burn out."

The boy shivered. "That *was* a narrow squeak," he said in awed tones. He turned. "I'll meet you where the portage enters the woods. So long, Noel."

"So long, Chris," came Noel's response.

CHAPTER 16

A FOREST FIRE

It was about four hours later that Chris, in company with thirty men recruited from Millville and the ridge, left the clearing and followed Noel Polchis down the tote-road leading towards the Keswick and Fish Lake. Immediately in front of Chris walked Sid Clowes, a pack on his back containing a blanket and food enough to last several days, and in his hand a long-handled axe. Each man was equipped likewise, though some, besides an axe, carried a spade and hoe. All were mildly excited. Richardson, the warden, had reported that another crew was coming in the following morning from Fredericton. Strange to say, Richardson seemed to have shaken off all signs of weariness. He swung along lightly behind Noel Polchis, walking, as did the Indian, with a slight inturning of his toes.

For a time, as the men walked, they exchanged local gossip, cracked jokes, and seemed as though they were going to a picnic rather than to take part in fighting a forest fire.

And now Chris was to see Noel Polchis exhibit his prowess as an expert woodsman. At the base of the opposite ridge, he suddenly turned off to the left, and disdaining all paths, led the way through a hardwood growth for a half-mile, passed round the base of a rocky pinnacle, and a few hundred yards farther on reached a wide portage.

Sid flung Chris a triumphant glance over his shoulder, and said: "The old chap's cut off a good three-quarters of a mile. This is the main portage. I could a done it, but not so quickly by fifteen minutes. Smell the smoke?"

Chris did smell the smoke. They were now in a small draw, or valley, and the air seemed much hotter than on the ridge. Under foot the red and yellow leaves of the maple and beech thickly carpeted the ground. They flushed numerous partridges, got several glimpses of the white flags of startled deer. Once they paused at a spring bubbling up from the base of a yellow birch. They unslung tin drinking cups and drank deep. Several of the men took advantage of the momentary respite to take off their jackets or sweaters, which they now either carried over their arms or stowed in their packs.

For another hour Noel led the way along the portage, then, without a word, he again branched off into the trackless woods. Chris glanced at the sun. It hung—a blood-red wafer—low on his left. His legs began to ache, but not for worlds would he have voiced his wish that he was at the end of his journey. No murmur had gone up from any one of the little band of firefighters. They plodded on, now quite silent, faces grimly set. Now and then one drew out a handkerchief or brushed a coat sleeve across a sweating brow.

Through a growth of spruce and cedar they followed Noel Polchis, their feet making no sound on the deep green moss; skirted a small pond, climbed the side of a hardwood ridge, up and ever up, until they reached the crest and paused for breath.

On the left loomed Lawrence Peak, and beyond it, northeast, dense clouds of smoke hid Fish Lake Mountain, and, fanned by a light wind, drifted southward. Straight ahead, in the valley below the band of men, could be seen a silver sheet of water, flanked on either side by a wide barren. "The Keswick deadwater,"[n] whispered Sid to Chris.

After five minutes' rest Noel again slipped the straps of his pack over his shoulders and once more led the way down the slope and into a dense growth of softwood timber. They clambered over fallen logs, moss-covered, where the boughs of trees met overhead, shutting out the sun, and long festoons of grey moss, like a patriarch's beard, hung idly in the breathless air. There they saw plentiful signs of animal life, beaten trails that ran hither and thither, the big hoof marks of moose, the daintier footprints of deer. Occasionally a rabbit bounded away or sat, its long ears nervously twitching, its startled eyes surveying the disturbers of its solitude; only the panting of men could be heard, a sharp indrawn breath as one slipped or stumbled over some projecting root, the soft dull pad of their feet.

In spite of his tired muscles, Chris was fascinated by this march through the forest; and his admiration for the man who led the way so unerringly grew into hero worship. Noel *was* wonderful. He couldn't understand how any man—even an Indian—could find his way with such perfect ease through a trackless wilderness. But Noel was doing it, and even the experienced woodsmen who followed him, occasionally muttered words of praise. The portage which they had left must be far to their left; Chris was quite sure of this, but no sooner had the thought come than, with, "Here we are," from Richardson, they suddenly stepped into a wide hauling or tote road. Chris turned to the man behind him. "What road is this?" he asked.

The fellow stared at him a moment, then said: "Why, it's the main portage to Fish Lake. Noel just cut off a mile and a half by coming across country."

"Thank you," said Chris.

The sun was now no longer visible. It had sunk behind the trees to the westward, and with its going a deeper silence seemed to pervade the forest. Little wisps of smoke filtered on the evening wind down the lane-like portage, stung the nostrils, made the eyes water.

A little farther on and Chris saw, ahead of them, a small clearing, and in the centre a couple of tumble-down log shanties. He saw Noel Polchis put down his axe, drop his pack before the door of the first shanty, to be followed by Richardson and those behind. This must be the place, then, where they were to stop the night. He was thankful, for his body was a-sweat; his feet were sore, his legs and shoulders ached.

As he slipped his pack off, Bob stepped forward, smiled, and patted him on the shoulder. "You've done splendidly, old chap," he said admiringly, "never a yip out of you."

Chris smiled back at him. "But I felt like yipping a score of times," he confessed. "But it was all wonderful, wonderful!"

The door of the old lumber shanty was now open. It smelled vile, though if any of the others were conscious of it they made no remarks. A low cooking stove, rusted with age, stood in the centre of the floor. At one end was a deal table, and the entire length of one side, a few feet from the floor, was taken up by a series of bunks covered with rotted spruce or fir boughs.

It was a memorable evening. By the flickering light of the candles they sat about the deal table and ate their supper and drank many cups of black, unsweetened tea; and then, when the food was cleared away to one end of the table, some of the men sat down again and played poker, for matches, while others sat on the Deacon seat,[39] and joked or told stories. And one got out a mouth organ and played haunting tunes to the accompaniment of many shuffling feet.

Now Noel slowly rose to his feet and went out of doors, followed by Richardson. A moment passed, then the latter poked his head in the door, beckoned with his hand to those inside. They crowded out into the camp yard, stared for some seconds in silence northward to where a red glow, as from a monster furnace, lighted up the sky. And as they gazed they could see tongues of flame suddenly shooting upward, as the fire claimed new victims; to their ears was borne a steady roar

---

39 A long bench running along the end of the bunks in a lumber camp.

and crackling, and every little while a prolonged crash as some monarch of the forest tore its way to earth.

Said Richardson: "Come boys, to our bunks; we've work to do at daybreak."

Chapter 17

Hard Work

When he awakened, he found all the others up, the fire snapping merrily in the stove and Mr. Clowes preparing breakfast. Lacing his boots he went outdoors, and joined several of the men who were gazing towards the scene of the forest fire and listening to Richardson's plans for combating it. To Chris it didn't seem much nearer than on the previous night. According to Richardson it would sweep—unless the wind should change—south-eastward, and, if not checked, endanger settlements along the railroad. Chris wondered how thirty men or even a thousand could successfully fight that monstrous conflagration. Could anything but water—a perfect deluge—stop its onward rush? He marvelled at the composure of these men beside him, their stolid assurance, and shivered as he followed Sid to the little spring brook a few yards beyond the shanty. The chips in the camp yard were slippery with frost; it covered the grass and Labrador tea bushes along the brook-side. As he cupped his hands in the icy water and conveyed it to his face, he gave vent to an involuntary, "Ouch!" and wondered how water could be so bitterly cold and not freeze. Sid, the water sparkling on his brown cheeks, paused to laugh at his discomfiture, then said: "Nothing like a wash in cold spring water to put the pep in you, old chap," and added significantly: "You'll sweat before the day's over, sure thing." He rubbed his face briskly with his towel, until it fairly glowed. Chris did likewise and ceased his shivering as the blood coursed through his veins.

"Smell the bacon fryin'?" said Sid. "Gee, I'm hungry as a bear! Come on, Chris," and the two lads broke into a run to the camp door.

Never had Chris tasted such strong tea. But no one else seemed to mind it, and he made no comment. The bacon was excellent, the bread and butter all that could be desired.

As soon as the meal was over, each man put up a lunch in his pack for the mid-day meal, for not until evening were they to return to the shanty. Then pipes were lighted, and each man, carrying his spade, or rake, or axe, again followed Noel Polchis through the woods along a tote road leading north-eastward.

For an hour, it seemed to Chris, Noel travelled this road; and now they were so near the fire they could feel its hot breath on the wind. The air was heavy with smoke and feather-like particles of burned boughs, which, so soon as they were touched by the hand, became a fine grey powder. They were now on a fairly open ridge covered with birch, maple, ash, beech, and balsams. The ground beneath their feet was several inches deep in dried leaves. Straight ahead, in the valley, vast volumes of smoke drifted south-east, showing the fire was, as Richardson had predicted, heading for the railroad. The ridge on which they were standing ran south, thence north-east, so Richardson planned to keep it confined to the valley, if possible. If they failed in their efforts and the fire swept over the ridge and got into the softwood in the draw on the other side, only a heavy rain would keep it from the settlement and the railroad. The fire ranger divided his crew, sending one party under Mr. Clowes north-eastward with directions to work westward and link up with the party under himself, which was to begin operations at the easterly base of the ridge on which they now stood. Should the wind shift, all were to hasten to the threatened quarter.

Now was Chris Alison to witness a strange passage of arms, between human beings and a forest fire which was gaining in fury as the wind hourly freshened. He saw the men strip to their undershirts, and, their brown hands clutching their weapons, go leaping down the ridge side towards that roaring furnace that was fast eating its way southward. With axes and hoes and rakes they strung out in a long line a bare two hundred yards from the green timber along the base of the ridge. Those with rakes began raking the dried leaves in windrows; came after them men with hoes and spades who dug a trench in the loamy soil. Those with axes cut down the balsams and flung them far from the trench line.

Chris, armed with a long-handled rake, worked beside Sid; a little way off, Bob and Noel Polchis, the former spading, the latter cutting away balsams and roots of trees that might make more difficult the efforts of the trench diggers. There was little conversation. They worked steadily and swiftly, realising that on their efforts much depended. This wilderness of trees was one of the chief assets, if not the greatest, the province boasted. Every acre of timber destroyed meant not only loss to the Government, but to each individual.

The sun was a great blood-red ball, and as it rose higher in the smoky sky the wind increased, and occasionally glowing sparks fell about the workers, caught in the leaves, sometimes behind them, sometimes at a distance up the ridge. Then would a man spring forward with a green branch from a balsam and beat it out.

Blisters began to come on Chris's hands, but he worked on doggedly, nor made any complaint. The sweat gathered on his brow, rolled down his face; his eyes smarted with the smoke; yet did he glory in this strange venture and wouldn't have gone back to the settlement if he could. He was here to do his bit—small though it might be compared with that of a grown man. That fire which was devouring great trees and small was a terrible enemy that must be fought. Thrills of excitement ran through his being. He felt that he was taking part in a great enterprise, one that called for generalship and stamina, and—yes, heroism, for, according to Noel and others of the men, often firefighters were driven to work for their very lives.

He had laboured for a couple of hours when Mr. Richardson called him and at the same time beckoned to Sid. "You youngsters come with me," he said. They followed him back along the ridge to where the lunch packs had been left. He picked up a couple of tin kettles, handed one to each of the boys, and, reaching for a third kettle, bade them accompany him.

"There's a spring brook on the other side of the ridge," he said. "I'll show you where it is, and you can carry water back to the men. They're about parched with thirst." He ceased, strode on ahead over the rise of ground, down the other side, and finally brought up in a thick growth of spruce and hemlock trees where, between banks of green moss, was a tiny brook. Flinging themselves on their knees, all three bent and drank long and deep. Oh, but it was refreshing! Chris felt that he could never have enough of it. Would he carry water back to the men labouring on the other side of the ridge? A thousand times yes. He dipped up a kettleful and followed Sid and Richardson back. The latter had taken out his sharp knife and was cutting strips of bark from the trees as he went. "All you've got to do is to follow the blaze on these trees," he cautioned, "and you can't go astray." He added a moment later: "The wind's freshening all the time," and muttered something beneath his breath which Chris didn't catch. But he, too, was conscious that the wind was much stronger. It tossed the branches of the trees about wildly, and their tops were filled with a strange clamour as of a thousand demons. Reaching the crest of the ridge again, they had a splendid view of the fire in the valley. No longer did the smoke billow lazily upward. It now swept southward in a mighty cloud. Tongues of flame sprang from tree to tree, shot upward with a wild crackling that sounded above the noise of the wind. Every moment a blazing top would snap off and be borne on the wind a hundred or more yards. The heat was oppressive.

Down the hill they hurried towards the men, who, when they saw them coming, dropped spade or axe or hoe and sprang forward, their parched lips framing exclamations of delight. The tin kettle passed from hand to hand down the trench line, and the "Thanks, sonny," "Oh, that was good!" "Boy, you're a lifesaver," were worth, thought Chris, a hundred journeys to the spring brook.

The morning passed; came noon and the men ceased work for a half-hour to eat their lunch and drink the inevitable cups of black tea, without which Chris was to learn no woodsman's meal was entirely complete. Then back again to the trench digging, which had now progressed well over the south-east slope within a hundred yards of the green wood. Now Richardson sent his axemen forward, and they began widening an old tote road that ran parallel with the path of the fire. On the other side Clowes and his crew were working towards them. Had they gauged things correctly—would the barrier be completed in time, or would the onrushing demon of destruction work its will before the two parties had linked up?—these were questions that Chris found men asking each other. He heard talk of "back firing,"[40] but this expedient was only to be used if it was found that they were in danger of being conquered. The wind was too strong, with such a small crew, to risk unnecessarily fighting fire with fire.

About three o'clock, however, a chorus of loud hurrahs from the ridge behind the workers heralded the coming of reinforcements. The number was not large, only twenty-five men and youths under Bradbury (chief fire ranger of the counties of York and Carleton) recruited from Millville and the surrounding settlements.

Bradbury, a small man, with steel-blue eyes, quickly took in the situation. "You've done well, Richardson," he said, "very well indeed."

---

40 Setting a fire along the inner edge of a fireline to consume the fuel
     in the path of a wildfire and change its direction [Wikipedia].

Richardson explained the plan of campaign. Bradbury listened, nodding his head nervously. "Fine," he said. "You've got a good trench here." He ceased, stamped on a cinder that came hurtling through the air and fell in the leaves at his feet. Then he turned to his men. "Come on, lads!" he cried, and led the way farther along the tote road, where soon was heard the heartening chop! chop! of their axes.

Until darkness began to fall Chris and Sid made journeys to the spring brook and brought back the life-giving water to the men. Often they discovered small fires beyond the trench line, and, picking up green branches, beat them out or called to the patrol man who had been detailed to watch for just such outbreaks.

That night Bradbury, with half a dozen men, camped on the ridge and ordered the balance of the fire-fighters to go back to the old logging camp for a night's rest. Mr. Clowes had not yet come over, and it was presumed that he would either come later or had possibly decided to make for a camp farther south. Chris would gladly have stayed with Bradbury and his men, but Bob advised him to go back and get some sleep. Said Sid: "If you're as tired as I am, you could fall asleep on a log, or the soft side of a rock. Come on, old chap!" So Chris went on, and before he had gone a quarter of a mile realised that he *was* tired, and sleepy; so tired indeed that his feet felt as though they weighed a ton, and so sleepy that he longed to curl up at the base of any one of those big trees and close his eyes. Darkness had settled over the forest long before they reached their destination, and he was quite sure that as soon as he struck camp he'd go to bed; he couldn't stay up a minute, not even to eat.

The wind had gone down. There was no sound save the thud, thud of his comrades' feet on the trail ahead and behind him, the rattle of a tin dipper in a pack, and, far off, the sound of a waterfall. Never had he felt such an overwhelming sense of isolation. His comrades—they were such a few—and the wilderness was so vast! Was it possible Noel Polchis was on the right trail? Would they go on marching, marching, stumbling along between these ghostly trees until dawn came? From out the black depths on their left a fox barked, and a little farther on came the snort of a deer, a loud crash, then silence. His heart thumped against his ribs. A few rods more and he saw a clearing, the low roof of the shanty they had left, oh such ages ago! It couldn't be the morning of this day!

And yet, tired as he was, when the fire was going merrily in the little stove and the bacon fried and tea made, he was quite ready to sit down at the deal table and eat heartily. Then did he crawl up into the log bunk and, his head on his arm, drift off to sleep. Only once during the night did he awaken to hear some one say, "Yes, your deal, Bill," and realised that some of the men were playing cards.

Chapter 18

Victory

When next Chris came back to consciousness, day had dawned. He wanted to close his eyes and again drift off to sleep, but Bob was calling him to get up and pulling at his foot, so reluctantly he crawled out. The smell of frying bacon filled the camp. Sid was helping arrange the tin plates and cups on the table, whistling merrily the while. "Hullo!" he said to Chris, adding, "You're some little old sleeper."

Chris yawned, nodded, shook himself, and going outdoors found that the smoke was thicker than on the previous day. It hung about the tops of the trees in thick clouds. There was no wind; no frost had fallen during the night, and the air was much warmer. The men were gathered in groups talking. He caught the words, "Bad—mighty bad. Polchis says rain, but I don't believe it. I wouldn't be in the chap's shoes who set this fire for a good deal if Bradbury or Richardson get hands on him." Then the boy went to the brook and washed. He heartily hoped that the person or persons responsible for the fire *would* be apprehended and punished. He couldn't understand how hunters could be so careless as to go away without making sure that their camp fire was quite out. As Richardson had said, the man who carelessly set fire to the forest, and the man who shot another in mistake for a deer or a moose, should be imprisoned. He sincerely hoped Noel was a sound weather prophet.

Going back to the camp, he sat down at the table and ate a hearty breakfast, then helped put up the midday lunch. A little later he was following the fire-fighters to the scene of the previous day's operations.

They found Bradbury and his half-dozen men already at work. All showed the effects of the night in the open. There had been frequent outbreaks of fire beyond the trench line during the first half of the night. Then the wind had gone down, and, making a pile of leaves in a hollow, they had a few hours' sleep.

And so the work of widening the tote road—cutting down brush and piling it—was again begun. Once in a while they could hear the sound of chopping on their right, and knew that it was Clowes and his crew working towards them. As the morning progressed, the air became suffocatingly hot. Then, about ten o'clock, a strong wind sprang up and blew the smoke and cinders straight into the faces of the workers. Word was passed down the line that Noel Polchis had again prophesied it would rain within twelve hours. All sincerely hoped so, but "the wind *had not shifted*", they argued, and until it did—

As yesterday, so now did Sid and Chris grasp their kettles, going back over the ridge to the spring brook, from whence they carried water to the workers. With hasty words of praise or thanks the kettles were snatched by blackened hands, conveyed to parched lips; the water gulped greedily; then the pail released to be carried to the next man along the line. There was a feverish activity in the way the men worked today, a tightening of the face muscles, an anxious look about the eyes that conveyed to Chris a repressed anxiety as to which would win out in this desperate combat; sharp commands echoed along the widening portage; men sprang eagerly to obey; jumped either to the right or left to dodge a tree on its earthward crash.

Towards noon the two lads had an adventure. Chris had just dipped up his kettle of water from the brook when, with a shout of alarm, Sid dropped his kettle and, breaking a branch from a small spruce tree, sprang down the hillside to where a volume of smoke was pouring from a pile of brush left by lumbermen the previous winter. Chris ran after him, threw his kettle of water (which had no effect whatever) on the blaze.

"Here," cried Sid, "take this!" and thrusting his spruce branch into his chum's hands, broke off another from a nearby tree and, swinging it about his head, began beating at the flames. Chris valiantly followed his example. But their efforts to subdue the fire were futile. With a rush and a wild crackling it sprang up a tall cedar, from the cedar to a spruce, leaped to a hemlock and shot with a roar to its very top.

For a moment the lads gazed dumbfounded on this new terror, then turned and ran back over the ridge, shouting for help as.they went. They reached the line of workers, shouted their news, and as with set faces the men raced towards the danger threatening their rear, the boys followed.

Now was Chris to witness and take part in a venture to which all that had gone before was as child's play. Instead of fighting fire at a distance of a half-mile, they now worked within a few rods of the flames. Bradbury threw his men in a cordon about the fire, and the sound of their axes, and the crashing of trees to earth, added to the roaring and crackling of the flames, sounded like a host at war. The sweat poured from the men's smoked-begrimed faces; they worked like demons, tearing at brush piles, beating savagely with green boughs at the flames. Flying cinders got in their eyes, down their necks.

What had been a tiny blaze a few minutes before was now a roaring furnace. Flames leaped from tree to tree, ran along the dry underbrush, caught in dried leaves, to eat their way to a green brush and soar upwards.

Chris was plying his spruce bough with all his strength, now here, now there. His hands were scratched and bleeding in several places, but with teeth grimly set, he worked on. Hoarse commands passed along the semicircle of men: the cry, "Heads up! 'ware there!" as a tree gave a warning crack and crashed to earth. Oh, if it would only rain!

One o'clock came, two. Instead of rain, the wind increased in volume. The fire leaped the barrier in a dozen places. With an oath, Bradbury ordered the men backward three or four hundred yards, and again they chopped and hacked to make a second barrier. Chris's throat was parched; great blisters rose on his hands; his cheeks burned as though they were on fire. Oh, for a drink of water—just a drop! But it was impossible now to get to the spring brook. It was in the centre of that wall of flame!

Suddenly, as they laboured, came a dull rolling sound from the heavens. What was that—dynamite? thunder? Was it possible—in October?... Again came that sound, nearer, then a sharp crash as though a monster shell had exploded beyond Lawrence Peak. Rain at last, thank God! Only a few drops at first, then, as crash after crash of thunder rolled and reverberated among the hills, it came in a perfect deluge.

Men ceased their labours and, led by Bradbury, retreated up the ridge. Some took off their felt hats, and catching the rain in the crown, eagerly drank it. For a few minutes they rested beneath whatever refuge they could find, then trekked back to the old lumber shanty; all drenched to the skin but quite happy. How it rained! It came in great blinding drops, and the thunder roared incessantly, and vivid chains of lightning stabbed the night-like day.

Chris, plodding doggedly behind Bob, shoulders hunched forward, was too happy to heed the water dripping steadily down his neck, or his knees and legs soaked from contact with the deluged shrubs that lined the trail. He had taken part in a great adventure, had fought his best. True, there had been times back there when he was almost dismayed, had felt that they were pitted against a foe that was unconquerable, but throughout it all he had not once feared for his own safety. Bob's words of praise to him and Sid back there on the ridge, "You young chaps did splendidly," rang gratefully in his ears.

They reached the camp, built a roaring fire in the stove, wrung out their drenched garments, nor heeded the raging elements outside. That rain was, as Bradbury gleefully remarked, in very truth worth a million dollars. No fire could withstand this deluge.

About nightfall Mr. Clowes and his crew of fire-fighters drifted in, tired and hungry, wet through, but happy also. Oh, the cups of hot black tea drunk that night, the gay jokes flung back and forth across the table! And then, when the things were cleared away, the cards were got out, and while the rain beat on the tarred roof above, they played the woodsmans' game—poker—until ten o'clock.

But before they crawled to their bunks, Richardson stood up and, his white head bared, his benevolent face lighted by the flickering candles, suggested that they should thank God for all His goodnesses. And while every head was bowed, his solemn and reverent voice rose in a prayer of praise and thanksgiving.

CHAPTER 19

WINTER DAYS

On the 15th of November came a light fall of snow. Chris was tremendously excited. He had visions of snowshoeing and sliding, of jingling sleigh bells; but before nightfall it had turned to rain, and on the following morning every vestige of snow had vanished. But on the next the wind blew strong from the north, and the nights were cold—so cold that the wheel tracks on the highway remained frozen until well on in the afternoons.

"You'll have all the snow you want and more," laughed Sid Clowes, when Chris suggested that perhaps there wouldn't be much snow this winter.

"You just wait until December," said Sid.

Day after day Chris, with his father and Bob, had been going down to the hardwood lot, near the lake, and chopping down yellow birch and rock-maple trees. Chris had pleaded to be allowed to use an axe. "You just watch me," he said; "I know how to do it." And he did, very well. He cut a deep notch, as he had seen the fire-fighters do, in the side of the tree, in the direction he wanted it to fall, then notched it slightly above, on the opposite side. Then, when the tree quivered and swayed, he pressed one shoulder against it and sprang quickly to one side, so that the butt, should it rebound, wouldn't strike him. "Splendid!" cried Bob; "you've got the knack of it, youngster." And with a satisfied nod his father remarked: "You'll do, lad. We'll have to send you into the woods with the lumberjacks next winter."

When eight or ten cords had been felled and limbed, the horses, attached to the low farm wagon, were brought down, and the logs hauled to the door-yard. Then the hardest, and to Chris the least interesting, of the work began. With a long cross-cut saw, himself at one end, Bob at the other, the logs were cut into stove wood lengths. These in turn were split with an axe and piled in a long tier for the sun and wind to dry.

But Chris had not to wait until December for a real Canadian snowstorm. On the morning of the 20th, when he awakened and looked from his window, he saw the ground and trees covered with white. And it was still snowing—millions upon millions of tiny flakes falling straight from the heavens. So thick they came that they almost shut out the lake and the opposite ridge.

Gleefully the boy dressed and went out into the kitchen, paused to receive his mother's welcoming smile and the words, "Well, laddie, you've got your snow at last," then stepped outdoors. Oh, but the air was good, and the snow crunched beneath his feet was not damp like the previous fall. Already it was up to his ankles. His eyes roamed over the hills; nothing but white—pure white met his eyes. He ran to the barn, watered and fed the stock, whistling merrily the while. Then back to the house again to brush the snow from his shoulders and warm his tingling fingers over the kitchen stove.

Never had the oatmeal porridge—covered with thick cream—tasted so good; and the bacon and eggs—the former not fried, but broiled to a crisp brown as only his mother could do it—were wonderful. He glanced at his mother's face, so flushed and contented looking. Yes, he was quite sure she was happy in this new land. In very truth it was now home to her, as it was to his father and Bob. As for himself, he knew for a certainty that never would he want to leave this place, save possibly for a visit, sometime, to the old land. In this land every few months brought some delightful transformation. Just think, only yesterday the leafless trees and brown hills, to-day the snow! True, for months to come, according to Sid, would be storm after storm. But what of that? It would be jolly, and, after a time, spring would come again.

After breakfast he followed Bob's example and put on a couple of pairs of home-knit woollen socks and drew over them the oil-tanned, moose-hide moccasins which he had purchased from the store at Millville. How light they felt after the thick boots he had been wearing all fall! He no longer wondered at many of the farmers wearing them the year round.

He went out to the barn and helped Bob milk the cows, then, so eager was he to be in the open—notwithstanding that it was still snowing—he walked out and down the road. And coming to the forest where the highway ended and the portage began, he tramped out this a half-mile, hoping to see the tracks of deer in the snow. But no deer tracks, nor that of any other animal, met his gaze. He wondered why. Had they moved farther back into the woods? But not until later did he learn that, during a storm, the woods creatures—and especially the deer—seldom travel. They were down in the thick swamps beneath the protecting branches of the spruce and cedar trees.

Never had he imagined that the woods could be so beautiful. Every branch and bush was laden with snow, and off up the side of the ridge the straight trunks of the yellow birch, beech, maple, and oak trees stood out sharply against the white background. Now a little wind was stirring. It made a strange crooning sound in the big hemlock on his right, rustled the dry leaves of some small beeches lining the portage, sent little avalanches of snow from the branches of the tall trees. Once again he wished that he were an artist, that he might paint the glory of these winter woods.

He reached the height of land, and regretfully turning, slowly retraced his steps. Suddenly he heard a sound, a bumping and banging off down the trail. It was the "toter" coming in. He walked on, and now, on the wind, he caught the tiny tinkling of bells that rose and fell, died away, to be utterly lost for a space of a few moments, and once again that bumping sound predominated.

He turned a bend of the portage and saw, topping a rise of ground, the heads of the horses, then the head and shoulders of Billy Stetson, the driver, seated on the high tote wagon.

He stepped to one side to let the tote team pass, noted, as it came nearer, that it was piled high with supplies—a barrel of flour, boxes of smoked fish, bags that looked like potatoes, several boxes of canned goods, a great jug of molasses, and, serving as a seat for the driver, a bale of hay for the horses—going in to the lumber shanty at the base of Lawrence Peak. For two weeks now Billy had been making three turns a week from Millville to the Peak.

The "toter" paused a moment to rest his horses and remark on the storm, then, lighting his pipe, he drove on. And for some moments—until distance swallowed the sound—Chris stood listening to those mellow notes of the bells and wondering if the people in distant cities knew of the vast amount of labour necessary to get out the lumber that went into the building of their homes.

The wind was now furiously beating the snow against his face, and breaking into a run, he soon reached the low ground. Here the spruce and balsams broke the force of the storm. He thought of those early adventurers: Champlain and De Monts. What hardships they must have undergone that first winter in this new world! Then there were no cities, no miles upon miles of land broken to the plough. All was a wilderness, inhabited only by the Indians and wild animals. His fancy skipped down the years. And yes—those bands of Loyalists who had landed in St. John and struggled up the river to cleave homesteads out of the virgin forest. How courageous they were, and how they suffered; leaving comfortable homes and acres because they must live under the British flag. That book of Raymond's° which his father had purchased, describing their coming, the privations of the men and women and children, he had now finished. They were heroes all. Then there were no railroads. Provisions for the winter must be laboriously transported by boat during the summer months over one hundred miles. Now the "iron horse" linked the most remote settlement to the seaports of St. John and Halifax and Montreal, and southward to the ports on the New England seaboard. What a change from a hundred years ago!

He reached the clearing. There was the smoke curling from the chimney of his home. Home? Small it was; but some day it would be enlarged; before Bob married the teacher, anyway. Good old Bob; sweet, earnest-faced Miss Allen. They would be so happy together!

The snow was now all of five inches deep, and it was still coming from the grey sky. If it snowed until nightfall, there would be at least ten inches of it. Then, ho for a deer hunt! It would be splendid tracking.

He leaped the fence and cut across the fields to home.

That night the weather cleared. The stars shone in the sky like great lamps, and a new moon flooded the fields and hillsides of white. It was all marvellously beautiful.

CHAPTER 20

THE DEER HUNT

The next morning the thermometer—which Chris's father had set up outside the kitchen door and every morning and evening for the last two weeks had religiously consulted—showed five below zero. That it could ever fall to thirty or even forty below zero seemed to him impossible.

Much to his wife's amusement, he was jotting down the varying degrees of temperature so that he could send them home to his brother.

Before Chris had finished breakfast, Sid Clowes entered, after a preliminary knock on the door, and, setting down the rifle he carried, announced to Mrs. Alison that he'd come to take Chris and Bob for a deer hunt. Bob regretted that he couldn't go. He was taking the horses out to the smith at Millville to be shod, and to bring back some groceries. Chris hastened through the remainder of his breakfast.

"You'll want plenty of socks on your feet, and a sweater under your mackinaw," said Sid, adding: "We may do a lot of standin' around. Still huntin's about as good a way as trampin' around a lot to get a deer."

Mrs. Alison turned to Sid: "You won't let him get lost?" she asked anxiously.

Sid chuckled. "Not on your life, Mrs. Alison. Why, even you could go in the woods after yesterday's storm and back track your way out. Besides," he added, "I know the lay of the land hereabouts, and even if there wasn't no snow, I could take a straight course home." He turned to Chris. "Better put a couple of pieces of bread in your pocket," he advised; "we mightn't get back until afternoon."

Chris buttoned his sweater about his throat, pulled on his mackinaw, got a handful of ball cartridges for the shot-gun, and announced that he was ready. He accompanied Sid to the door, then turned back to put some matches in an inner pocket. Before the day was over he was thankful that he had done so.

Side by side the two lads struck across the fields, and entered the woods practically at the same spot which Chris had taken eight months before when first he met Noel Polchis. He wondered what Noel was doing now. He must make up a package of tobacco and mail it to his friend for Christmas.

Numerous rabbit tracks led here and there through the snow. Near the head of the lake they crossed what Sid said was an otter track. It looked to Chris as though someone had dragged a log through the snow. But Sid was sure it was made by an otter. "If you followed it, you'd find it led to a hole in the ice," he said. Suddenly he stopped and pointed to the hoof marks of a deer. "It's a buck too," he whispered. "Too big for a doe. But it isn't fresh; made last night, probably."

A little later they came on two more tracks: one large, one very small. Farther on they saw where the buck had joined the others, and all had proceeded along the tote road for a hundred yards, stopping at times to feed. Soon the tracks along the tote road ceased. Sid pointed to his left, signifying to Chris that they had probably gone over the hardwood ridge.

For a time the forest was wondrously still. The boughs of the trees drooped with their weight of snow. Then, far off to the right, a tinge of gold heralded the rising sun. A squirrel began a lively chatter in a beech tree ahead of them; a red-capped woodpecker hopped, head foremost, down a dead fir tree trunk in a succession of staccato "tut!—tut! tut! tuts!" that made the forest ring. A big owl swooped with a whir of wings from a tall hemlock and disappeared into the low land on the right.

Where the portage swings round the base of the hardwood ridge, Sid branched off and, followed by Chris, slowly began to climb the incline to the crest. Chris noted that Sid walked warily, was careful not to step on any brush, and that his eyes roved from side to side. Deer tracks were now plentiful; indeed, so plentiful that it was difficult to determine which way they led. In several places the snow was pawed up and beech leaves overturned, showing that either during the night or that very morning they had been feeding here.

On the south-eastern slope of the ridge, beside a big spruce that had blown down in a late wind, Sid stopped. "You wait here," he whispered to Chris. "You can sit down, if you want to." He brushed the snow from the trunk of the tree. "You can see for seventy-five yards. Just stay quiet and keep your eyes peeled; I'm going back along the tote road and work north, over the ridge. Like as not I'll drive something down to you. And"—he paused a moment—"if you shoot, shoot straight, but don't shoot at anything that isn't a deer."

Chris nodded. He knew that Sid meant: "Be sure it isn't a human being you're shooting at." A story of John Richardson's— about a chap who'd shot his brother in mistake for a deer— he would never forget. Yes, as the old fire-ranger had bitingly remarked: "A man hasn't got four legs, nor horns; and it's only a darn fool that shoots at a bush movin', 'cause behind the bush might be a human bein'."

He watched Sid disappear over the hill towards the portage, then broke off some small boughs from a nearby fir, laid them on the fallen tree trunk, and sat himself down. His half-hour walk had set him perspiring, so he opened his coat to let in some air. Straight ahead was a small beech-tree covered plateau, with an occasional spruce and balsam, their boughs weighted down with snow. Beyond, the ground rose to a small pinnacle that ran in a horseback[41] up the side of the ridge. Between this and the plateau was a narrow cut, or valley, that, from the direction it took, Chris decided must lead down to the softwood on his right.

Back and forth over the plateau the lad's eyes had roamed. He craned his neck about and took in the slope behind him, but not a sight nor sound of any living thing had he seen or heard save a squirrel that had ventured out to revel in the sunlight. Chris hoped the little beggar had a good supply of nuts tucked away in some hollow tree or log. Down in the softwood a partridge drummed. Far off, southward, a locomotive whistled.

Despite the fact that he had on two pairs of woollen stockings beneath his moccasins, his toes began to tingle uncomfortably. He wanted to stamp them on the ground, but that would make a noise, so he wriggled them until the unusual exercise caused them to cramp. Again his eyes searched the plateau, picking out space after space between the tree trunks; then he began all over again. This "still" hunting was rather uninteresting sport, he decided. And yet, according to Noel Polchis, who should know, it was, if persisted in, sure to bring results sooner or later. But it was slow nevertheless. One must be possessed of a vast amount of patience to "still" hunt in one spot, like Noel, for hours at a time. Thinking of Noel set his mind to recollecting some of the Indian words Noel had taught him. He recalled quite a number, including: *O-ast*, which meant snow; and *K-tak-miq*, earth; *O-kin-o-sis*, boy. And how his tongue stumbled over that long Melicete term for rice: *Ab-tel-mol-tine-oeial. Kam-no-kik*, England, the land of his birth. He felt quite elated at remembering so many. Noel, he knew, would be pleased when, coming the following spring to hunt

41 A low and somewhat sharp ridge of gravel or sand; a hog-
   back [OED].

muskrats, he found his pupil had not forgotten. The boy remembered the day after the fire, when, trekking back to the settlement, Noel had gathered up his traps, and with *"Adiou, Chris, I come next spring,"* accompanied the fire-fighters from Millville over the ridge to catch the train. Two things the boy would never forget: the night when Noel with his birch-bark horn called the big bull moose out on the moonlit barren, and those hours north of Lawrence Peak fighting the forest fire.

Something, no bigger than his hand, passed before his vision away off there between the trees on the very crest of the horseback. His fingers nervously clutched the barrel of his gun. He strained his eyes until they ached. He was quite sure something had moved. Must have been a bird—one of those slate-winged moose birds, possibly, or a sparrow. Perhaps—but no—it couldn't have been snow falling from a tree, because what had passed the corner of his eye was dark. Sid? It might be that his chum was working down that side of the ridge.

Whatever it was, had instantly disappeared, and, now that his momentary excitement was over, he was again conscious of his cold toes and that his back, between his shoulders, was like ice. A few minutes more and he'd take a short walk across the plateau and back. It would set his blood circulating.

Suddenly, just over the near side of the cut, he saw what looked like the forked branch of a tree moving. But trees didn't move of their own volition; and there was no wind, not a breath. Again his hands clutched his gun, and, drawing it up over his knees, he waited. He was conscious that his heart was beating so loudly that it seemed as though it were not his heart, but the sound of someone or something running. The thing that looked like the branch of a tree was now no longer visible, and he wondered if, in Sid's words, he were not "seeing things." Just for a moment he closed his eyes, then opened them, looked, and there, not thirty yards distant, stood a magnificent buck, head on, calmly surveying him.

The boy lifted the gun to his shoulder, sighted his eye along the barrel straight for the deer's neck, then his finger pressed the trigger. There was no answering report. The buck, his great antlers upflung, still stood as though carved in stone, his forefeet planted wide apart, the warm breath from his distended nostrils curling above his head.

Chris felt his knees trembling; the gun in his hands was behaving amazingly, bobbing up and down, to the right and to the left, anywhere but on a line with the deer's neck. With a masterful effort he steadied it, again pressed the trigger. No response, no thundering discharge. He glanced down, saw with chagrin that he had failed to cock it, and snapped the hammer back.

At the metallic sound the buck sprang away a dozen yards, stood for one thrilling second broadside, then, almost, it seemed, on the very instant Chris pressed the trigger and the answering discharge thundered in his ears, the buck coursed down over the hillside—a dun-coloured streak—and was lost to view in the thick growth at the foot of the ridge.

"Missed!" muttered Chris; "a clean miss!" and realised that he had experienced buck fever. Wouldn't Sid laugh when he told him. Well, the buck was gone. But oh, what a beauty! Such a splendid set of antlers.

He walked over to where the deer had stood facing him. My, what a magnificent leap he had made! He paced it off— eleven feet! What was that in the snow? A spot of blood? Yes— there was another, and a great splotch on the white bark of a birch tree. Possibly he had hit the deer a mortal blow, and it was now lying down there near the green wood. Ejecting the empty shell, he replaced it with ball cartridge and started down the incline.

At the bottom, in a little clearing where were leafless raspberry bushes, he saw where the deer had fallen and got up again. A tiny trail of blood led straight into a tangled undergrowth;

and here he lost the crimson trail, nor was he again able to pick it up. But after hunting about for some time, he saw what he took to be the buck's hoof marks. They were large and of recent make, and he followed on, winding between tree trunks and through tiny clearings half-grown up with laurel and Labrador tea shrubs, hoping at every turn to find the buck lying dead. True, there was now no sign of blood, but the creature might be bleeding inwardly.

Once he thought he heard someone shout. He gave an answering call, but receiving no reply, decided his ears had deceived him. The growth through which he was now making his way was much thicker and all green wood, from which hung great festoons of moss, powdered with snow. Straight ahead was a monstrous pine tree towering high above its fellow spruce. It made him think of John Richardson's pine and the man who had laid it low.

The forest seemed much darker. He glanced up for the sun, and was surprised to find it was not visible; the sky was overcast with lead-coloured clouds. "Of course," he thought, "the settlement is over there to my right, and anyway, all I've got to do is to back-track to reach the ridge again." A little farther and he'd turn back. It would be disappointing to have to tell Sid he'd made a mess of things, but the lengths of the tracks ahead showed that the buck was still going strong. Possibly after all it had been a light flesh wound.

Suddenly, ahead of him, he saw fresh moccasin tracks. Could Sid be down here? He called, and getting no response, broke into a run. Perhaps a hundred yards he went, then stopped, a feeling of doubt and amazement in his heart. There, directly ahead of him, loomed a big pine that looked for all the world like the same tree he had passed fifteen minutes before. But it couldn't be. That other pine was over on his right. He took off his cap and wiped his perspiring brow. He was about to follow the tracks past the tree, but stopped again as the thought flashed on him that this *was the same pine* he had passed a short while before, and that he had merely travelled in a circle and come back to it. He remembered that first morning—so long ago now—when he had been turned around in the bit of woods between the brook and his father's field. He could follow his tracks back now or stay right where he was until Sid came to him. But no need of that. He was sure, oh yes, absolutely sure, that all he had to do was to turn at right angles, travel straight, and he'd be back to the ridge in no time.

Taking off his mackinaw, he flung it over one arm and, his gun under the other, broke into a run. For perhaps ten minutes he hastened on and came to what he saw was a cedar swamp. He made a detour, clambered over fallen logs, burst through dense thickets, scratched his face and hands, ripped his clothes. It had begun to snow again; a wind sprang up, droning through the trees weirdly. In five minutes the flakes were so thick he had difficulty to see more than a few yards. Again that feeling of bewilderment crept into his heart. No longer was he sure he was going in the right direction. He was lost—lost in the big forest in a blinding snowstorm! He remembered his mother's admonition to Sid not to lose him. What would befall him? With feverish haste he cocked the gun, fired both barrels into the air, then thrust in two more cartridges and fired again. Now in a perfect panic, he started to run straight into the face of the storm. His heart was pounding painfully, the perspiration and melting snow dripping from his brow half-blinding him. At length, exhausted, he brought up against a fallen spruce, barking one knee against a protruding branch.

Then reason came to his befogged brain. He sat down and tried to think things out. He was lost, sure enough. No use now to attempt to back-track. His tracks were already so filled with snow that he wouldn't be able to determine which way they led. It was still early in the day. Sid would follow him up and must, sooner or later, find him. But what if Sid didn't come and he

had to stay out all night? He must make some sort of shelter
and collect some firewood. He thanked God he had brought
matches. Standing his gun against a tree, he took out his knife
and cut off, close to the ground, a small moose-wood sapling.
This, with a piece of cord from his mackinaw pocket, he securely
lashed to a couple of maples which stood, about four feet apart,
a short distance from the fallen log. Now he cut several spruce
boughs and, setting one end in the snow, allowed the other to
rest against the improvised ridge pole, overlapping them one
upon the other, until he was sure no particle of snow would
penetrate. When this was all done to his satisfaction, he cut
and broke more boughs, spreading them inside on the floor of
his camp.

The finding of firewood was more difficult. He didn't dare,
after his late experience, go far away from his camp site, and
lacking an axe, he must entirely depend on such dry branches as
he could break from the surrounding trees. Yet, after an hour's
work, he had quite a little pile.

Instead of abating, the storm had increased in violence, the
wind whistling and moaning through the trees like a creature in
pain. He crawled beneath his rude shelter and, knees up-drawn,
gazed ruefully at the whirling flakes. He felt hungry, and taking
out the few slices of bread he had put in his pocket before
leaving the house, undid the parcel, and, limiting himself to one
slice, ravenously ate it. He thought of home, of his parents and
Bob, of the anxiety they would feel should Sid not find him.
What an ass he had been to get lost! In a little he would collect
more fuel, and, should he have to spend the night here, he would
be able to keep warm. On the morrow—of course—the sun
would shine, and he would travel slightly to the right of it, as Sid
had once advised him, and soon strike the portage. He wondered
why Sid hadn't fired his gun in answer to his own frenzied
firing. Was it possible that his chum was lost too? He felt in
his pocket, drew out the last remaining cartridge, was about to

put it in the gun and discharge it, when the thought came to him that, should he do so, and Sid failed to hear and come, he would not only be defenceless against possible wild animals, but have nothing to kill even a rabbit to keep himself from starving. He knew not what to do. The firing of that cartridge might bring Sid to him within a few minutes; but then, what if Sid didn't hear it? Should he take the hazard, gamble his last cartridge on the chance that Sid was within hearing distance? He sat there, the cartridge in the palm of his mittened hand, his brain flooded with indecision.

Suddenly there bounded down the trail he had lately made an animal different from any he had ever seen. Opposite him, and but a few feet distant, it stopped, drew back on its haunches and, its bright eyes fastened on him, bared its long white teeth in a snarl that sent a shiver of fear over his body. For a few moments he gazed spellbound on that big, cat-like form, noted the short, pointed ears, the tufts of hair on either jaw; then he shoved the cartridge into the breech, snapped it to, and, as he cocked the piece, ran his eye along the sight and pulled the trigger. For one bewildering moment he knew not whether he had hit the thing or missed. He saw it give a wild leap into the air, heard a bloodcurdling yell, then, as he sprang to his feet, his gun clubbed to give further battle, he saw the creature rolling over and over in the snow, biting at its body with its teeth, finally to roll over and lie still.

From somewhere behind him, far away, he heard a shot—a rifle shot, he was quite sure. Could it be Sid? He shouted as loud as he could shout again and again. Then listened. Came only the sound of the wind. He waited. Again the report of the rifle. Oh, for another cartridge to make answer! He shouted himself hoarse. He forgot the dead animal. His whole being was strained to catch an answering shout. He felt sure it must be Sid who was firing. Would it be safe to start through the woods in the direction of the sound? Hardly. Sid might have exhausted his cartridges, and in trying to reach him he might go farther away. No, the best thing for him to do was to stay where he was. Feverishly his hands raced through his pockets in the hope that he had overlooked a shell. Alas! there was not one, and, disappointed, he began shouting again, pausing after every effort to listen.

The minutes passed slowly. A couple of trees, one leaning over against the other, rubbed together with an odd, eerie sound. The snow was now coming in driving flakes, that lashed his face and eyes so that they pained. The pile of branches he had collected was buried with snow.

Suddenly, his heart leaped. "Whoo-hoohoo! Whoo-hoo—hoo, Chris!" came the call. Sid's voice! Chris sent back a joyous shout, and in a few minutes Sid burst upon him, his coat off, his face as red as a berry. He mopped his streaming brow with his handkerchief. "Oh, golly! golly!" he ejaculated over and over. "You did give me a scare." Then he suddenly sat down and gazed speechlessly up into Chris's face.

"I—was lost," ventured Chris.

Sid nodded. "I guess you were," he said, was silent a moment; then, with a jerk of his thumb towards the tiny lean-to, "*You— you made that?*" he demanded.

"Yes," admitted Chris hesitatingly. "I thought I'd better have some sort of shelter if I had to stop the night. I gathered a little pile of wood too."

"Oh, golly!" said Sid; "you've got some sense—more'n I thought for a green'un. Most of 'em would've gone runnin' here and there till dark come on." He paused a moment, then asked: "But why didn't you back-track after you killed the buck?"

"Killed the buck?" queried Chris. "Oh, Sid, but I didn't; I just wounded it. I followed—"

"Shucks!" exploded Sid. "It's layin' dead back there at the foot of the ridge; dead as a door nail—ten points—a beauty. It'll dress a hundred and fifty pounds."

"But," interjected Chris, "I followed its trail into the green woods a long distance after I'd wounded it—"

"Huh!" broke in Sid, "you followed another buck. I tell you, you got your buck through the lungs. He's back there at the foot of the ridge. I—" He paused, went on: "Just after I heard your first shot, I started a buck over the other side of the ridge; just got a peep at him. I thought you'd be all right, so I followed him, and at last got a shot—"

"Did you get him?" demanded Chris.

"Yes," answered Sid modestly, and continued: "I bled him, then walked over to where I'd left you—" He paused again, gave Chris a quick look, then, rising, said: "Come on, old boy; I'll show you your buck, then we'll go out and get Father to come in with the sled."

"But, Sid," cried Chris, "look here, I shot something else."

"Where? What?" demanded Sid, looking about him.

For answer Chris walked over and catching the snow-covered animal by one paw, dragged it a few feet towards his chum.

"Holy Moses! A bob-cat! Oh, gee, a whopper!" cried Sid excitedly. "Oh, boy, you're some little old hunter. Why, Chris, you've got a cat there that's worth ten dollars."

"Ten dollars?" echoed Chris.

"Um!" nodded Sid. He was feeling about the animal with his hand. "You got him in the neck, old scout." He rose, pulled out his hunting knife. "We'll take the insides out of him so he won't be so heavy to carry," he said. "Catch hold there of his hind legs, Chris. There, that's right." He ran the sharp blade into the bob-cat's thick hide, and Chris, noting every movement of the knife, watched his companion disembowel the creature, then tie a piece of cord about the fore and hind legs, holding them together. Through this Sid passed a sapling. Bidding Chris put one end over his shoulder, he did likewise with the other end. And thus, the bob-cat swinging from side to side between them, the two lads—Sid leading the way—trudged through the deep snow, and in an incredibly short space of time had reached the tote road that led round the base of the hardwood ridge.

"You see," said Sid, "you weren't such a long distance away after all. You just got down in that softwood and travelled in a circle. Come, old chap, your buck lies over there. I'll show you what a beauty he is, then we'll hustle back to the house, get Father to come with the horse and the light sled. Won't they all be surprised? Two bucks and a bob-cat aren't so bad for one mornin's hunt, eh?"

Chris nodded, followed his companion up the slope and down the other side until they reached the raspberry thicket where he had lost the blood trail—it seemed now so long ago. Here Sid turned abruptly to the left, stopped behind an old blow-down, pointed to where, half-covered with snow, the deer lay outstretched. "There he is, old chap. Ten points. He'll dress one hundred and seventy-five pounds," said Sid, taking hold of the antlers and holding the head up to Chris's admiring gaze.

"I hope yours is as big," said Chris.

Sid shook his head. "Mine's a baby alongside of this," he replied, and there was no trace of jealousy in manner or words. "We won't bother going over to where mine is," he said. "It's a good mile." He pulled out his watch. "It's one o'clock; by the time we get Dad and are back here again, it'll be late afternoon. Let's beat it, Chris."

They "beat it" back over the ridge and on to the portage, where their tracks, made earlier in the morning, were now entirely obliterated. Down the little inclines they went, slipping, sometimes falling, but with gay shouts and laughter. The wind whistled and groaned in the great trees, and the snow whirled ceaselessly from the leaden sky. So thick did it come that when they reached the clearing their shoulders and caps were covered.

Far ahead of them Howland Ridge rose white against the sky. No track of man or sled led over its summit. Indeed, all that marked the highway was the snake fence of cedar rails zigzagging over the hill.

"I'll just run home and tell Mother and Father the luck we've had," said Chris. "I'll be with you in ten minutes."

"Better have a cup of tea," Sid advised. "I'll wait. I need one myself."

Chris climbed the fence, struck off happily across the fields towards the log house from whose broad chimney the smoke bravely swirled to meet the snow-filled air. And as he went the lad's heart was filled with thanksgiving that he was safely approaching his home.

He reached the door, brushed the snow from his legs and body, lifted the latch, stepped in. His mother was sitting in the rocking-chair before the fire, knitting at a sock and reading from an open book in her lap—a book which, with a smile, he noted was *David Copperfield*. A few feet away, his father, the smoke from his pipe curling above his grey head, was sitting at the table writing a letter to the brother in the old land. What a cheery scene! The fire crackled merrily. The tea-kettle sang a bubbling song of joy. The cat and her two kittens lay sprawled contentedly close to its diffusing warmth. On the sideboard stood three or four brown loaves of freshly-baked bread, a couple of pies, and a big bowl of doughnuts.

Home! A feeling of perfect contentment filled the lad's heart. His mother looked up, smiled on him. "I'm so glad you're back, Chris, lad," she said; "I was beginning to worry."

His eyes dwelt lovingly on her sweet, lined face. What a brick she was! And then he told her of his adventures.

The storm ceased about four o'clock. Mr. Alison went out and with a rule measured the depth of snow, then appended to the letter he had begun to his brother earlier in the day:

"Fourteen inches of snow in the door-yard, Jim. It reminds me of Blackmore's *Lorna Doone*. Do you remember the big storm he describes and how John Ridd went out and rescued the sheep from the drifts? The temperature is dropping too. I wonder what it will be like at twenty or thirty below? Not so bad, I fancy. A dry cold that sets the blood tingling through one's veins—even mine, old thing.

"From the window I can see neighbour Clowes, his son, and Chris entering the yard with the buck and wild cat I mentioned earlier in this. The boy looks happy. He has informed me of his wish to spend next winter in the lumber woods. I don't know—it will be hard work. And yet, might it not be a valuable experience? This section of the country is rich in timber of all kinds and, who knows, some day, if he has the pluck, he may climb high!"

THE END

Editor's Afterword

The book

Chris in Canada is rooted in a particular time and place: Howland Ridge, New Brunswick, in the early 1920s—a century ago, when George Frederick Clarke (GFC) first knew it. The details of farming belong entirely and precisely to the period and the place.[42] *Chris in Canada* can function as a historical snapshot of life on Howland Ridge in the early1920s—possibly in exactly 1920.[43] The immigrants have travelled to the ridge by ship, train and finally farm wagon; cars are not unknown, but they are rare. People who live on the ridge often stay there for considerable periods without visiting even the village of Millville, three miles away. They trade eggs with a pedlar for groceries and dry goods; they get milk and butter from their own cows. They don't have telephones. Horses, not tractors, draw their farm equipment and twitch logs out of the woods. Women and girls wear ankle-length skirts; men and boys put on hats or caps whenever they go outdoors.[44] Children go to the one-room schoolhouse on the ridge.[45]

---

42 For instance, it is full of distinctively New Brunswick words, some of which I have noted in the page notes.

43 In the chapter "Harvest-home" the threshers arrive on "Wednesday, the 15th of September." September 15th fell on a Wednesday in 1920. (It also fell on that day in 1915 and 1926, but 1915 is too early—*Chris* is not set during the Great War—and 1926 is too late, since the book was with the publisher by late 1924.) But GFC could be cavalier with dates; it is possible that he did not have 1920 in mind when he wrote "Wednesday, the 15th of September."

44 All that was a century ago, and Howland Ridge has changed—but less than many places in central New Brunswick. GFC's home town of Woodstock has changed far more. The ridge road is still gravel; and there are still farms along it, though some of the houses on the lower slopes belong to professionals who commute to Fredericton.

45 It is still there, disused but in good condition, at least externally.

But the reason that *Chris in Canada* stayed in print from 1926 to the early 1950s lies not in the accuracy of its details, but in its timeless quality and its breadth of human appeal. GFC had returned, for the first time since his early river-driver stories, to the themes that were to inspire his best writing for the rest of his life: the country, the woods, and the people who lived and worked in them. *Chris in Canada* is the simplest kind of story—this happened, then that happened: almost plotless, structured by the changing seasons; not highly exciting (except for the forest fire), but deeply satisfying. Noel is the older friend and mentor that children long for as they move into adolescence. Chris himself is what many girls and boys through the ages have wanted to be: brave, honest, adventurous. Young people can see themselves in him and live in imagination through his first year in a new land.

Chris has his creator's serious nature, mixed with his high spirits and his love of wilderness adventure. The book is not autobiographical, but GFC's own experiences run through it like a thread. Here are a few instances. In his youth, like Chris, he read stories from an old *Boys' Own Annual*. Like the berry-picking boy from Maple Ridge, he loved bananas. When he describes how Chris and Bob find themselves so close to a cow moose that they can see "the long lashes flickering over her small black eyes," he is probably recollecting the time he foolhardily called a cow moose and had to climb a tree to escape.

> She came over quite close, so that—actually, I could have counted the lashes on her eyes. She kept me there for an hour and a half, before she finally turned and slid—I say slid, because that was her motion—she slid away into the alders.[P]

I don't know whether he ever fought a forest fire. Perhaps not, since he never spoke of it, but he had second-hand experience, which for a writer can be enough. He gleaned some insight into firefighting on a trip to Ayers Lake in 1911, when he, his sister and his fiancée shared a cabin with rangers who had been fighting a fire on Sow-Back Mountain. It was possibly the fire Noel tells Chris about—a fire so bad that it drove the fighters into Ayers Lake, where moose and deer joined them: "Black bear come in lake too, with cubs; never mind us; come up close." Noel's account probably reminded GFC of a story he heard from from his own grandfather, who as a child lived through the great Miramichi fire of 1825. The settlers waded into the Miramichi with their children in their arms, while "moose, bear and other wild creatures crowded in beside them."[q]

GFC, Howland Ridge and Taffa

GFC first saw Taffa in 1905, from the top of Howland Ridge. He wanted to go down to the lake, but he was with friends on a hunting trip to Trout Lake, and they had to get there before dark. For the next fifteen years he tramped over the wilderness described in this book, and acquired hunting camps on Ayers Lake and the Northeast Lake Deadwater. But he didn't visit Taffa till one day in the summer of 1920. He was enchanted. The camp on the point was for sale, and he bought it. For the next forty years he and his family stayed at Taffa every summer for a week, two weeks, three; in the spring and fall he stayed there on hunting trips with friends, till he stopped hunting in the early 1930s.

Howland Ridge and the lake entered into his imagination. In one of his poems he asks not to be buried in "a formal grave" when he is dead:

> Nay, put me rather in a spot I know
> O'er Howland ridge; I've loved the place full well
> These many years, in summer and in snow...[r]

He set several animal stories at Taffa; and he described the farming people of the ridge in two books for young people (*Chris in Canada* and *Chris in the Wilderness*), two unpublished novels, and a short story. He knew the ridge dwellers as well as an outsider could, and he cared about them. When I was a child, we always stopped in Millville on the way to Taffa, to see Mr Flemming, who had once farmed on the ridge.[s] My brother and I would sit kicking our heels against the sofa, impatient to get to the lake, while GFC exchanged reminiscences with the old man.

The Flemmings had lived on the ridge for generations;[46] they were not the originals of the fictional Alisons. Neither were the Connors—the family whom we knew best during my lifetime. They emigrated from England[47] in 1925—two years *after* GFC wrote *Chris in Canada*. Their first farm was at Hawkins Corner; they only moved to Howland Ridge in about 1929.[t] Charles and Maud Connor were nearly fifty when they arrived in Canada. Mr Connor was tall, straight-backed and grizzled, with piercing eyes and a big moustache; his wife was tiny and delicate. They lived on the last farm on the ridge before the road narrowed to a track and entered the woods.

I last saw them in 1971. We stood inside the screen door of their tiny shingled farmhouse while Mr Connor told us how they came out from England "in nineteen twenty and five," first to Millville, then to this place at the back of beyond. He didn't say, though GFC often did, that the government had promised immigrants good farmland, not the marginal hill farm that they allotted to the Connors. Nor did the Connors get the $600 the government had promised them.[u]

----

46 There used to be a tiny family cemetery on the ridge, with a sign, "Flemming Cemetery," and a few weathered gravestones. It was there till about 2010, but by 2018 it was gone. The headstones must now be in the Hawkins Corner cemetery.

47 It was their second emigration. They had first moved to England from County Westmeath in Ireland, where they were Protestants in a Catholic area, to escape the sectarian warfare of the early 1920s.

Who then were the originals of the Alisons? I have looked through the 1911 and 1921 census records without finding a family of recent immigrants living on Howland Ridge,[v] though I did find a few such families elsewhere in the area. GFC might have known one of them—or he might not: he may have had no specific model for his fictional family. He was writing about Canadian farm life for young English readers, so he drew them into the story by making his leading character a young English immigrant. He set the book on Howland Ridge because he knew several of its farming families and had paid close attention to their characters, their lives, and the details of their labour, which fascinated him. He knew and loved the wilderness that stretched beyond the ridge further than the eye could see; and he knew and loved Noel Polchies, who hunted, fished and trapped in its woods and streams. He didn't need to know a particular immigrant family to write convincingly about one boy's introduction to that rural and wilderness world.

Millville, Howland Ridge, Taffa: a historical note

Millville was founded in about 1860, as a settlement of the New Brunswick and Nova Scotia Land Company.[48] By 1871 it had a post office and a population of 300;[w] by the turn of the century it had a railway station, a hotel, a sawmill, a cheese factory, a carriage factory, and five stores. It had become the commercial centre of a substantial rural district—though, on the evidence of this book, farming families also bought or bartered goods from the pedlars who plied the country roads of the province as late as the 1920s. (In 1921 GFC's wife and sister rode some of the way with an old pedlar on their epic hike from Woodstock to Fredericton.[x])

---

48 A British company. It bought large tracts of Crown land cheaply, divided it into lots and sold them to Canadian and immigrant farmers.

The NB and NS Land Company founded the Howland Ridge settlement in 1875. It seems to have taken its name from two of the early settlers, Solomon and Alexander Howland.[y] The settlement remained rural; it had a one-room schoolhouse, but no store.

From the early nineteenth century onward, the Canadian government was desperate for immigrants, especially farmers. The Land Company was one of many schemes that the federal and New Brunswick governments encouraged—and subsidised, with assisted passages, grants of farmland (and often farmhouses), and money for setting-up expenses and farm equipment.[z] In return, the immigrants had to promise to stay on the land for a period of years.[49] After World War I the British government joined in a number of these schemes, hoping to alleviate unemployment at home by sending large numbers of ex-soldiers to the Dominions. Governments and land companies alike often promised more than they gave, as in the Connors' case.

Taffa Lake is called Taffy Lake on maps and in present-day local usage, but GFC insisted that Taffa was the correct name;[50] he said it was a Maliseet word. It is likely that he got the information from Noel Polchies.[51]

---

49 To discourage them from moving to cities—or going to the States straight from the ship that had brought them to Canada.

50 Interestingly, in his short memoir *Quest for Gold*, Charles Connor's son Robert calls the lake Taffa nine times (adding a couple of times that it is locally pronounced Taffy), but Taffy just once. I assume that in calling it Taffa he reflects a usage that was still current among older locals.

51 GFC spelt the name as "Polchis" in *Chris in Canada* and *Chris in the Wilderness*, but "Polchies" after the 1920s. Likewise, in his later books he often spelt Noel's first name as "Noël".

Noel Polchis

Noel Polchis was born around 1860 and died in 1927. He had been GFC's mentor and dear friend for twenty years. Like most First Nation men of his time (and later times), he worked at a number of trades, both for others and on his own. He hunted, fished, and trapped. He made baskets and probably barrels: his occupation is listed as "cooper" in the 1921 census. He worked as a hunting and fishing guide. His grandson Peter Paul said:

> …he was like all the other Indians, he made snowshoes, and summers he worked on the river drive, spring of the year he went driving lumber out [of the woods][aa]

Speaking of Noel's influence on his grandson, the ethnographer Nicholas Smith said:

> …[Peter] was one of the last Maliseet to experience a hunter's life style. He was lucky to learn hunting from one of the best hunters and trappers on the Reserve.
> He grew up with conservative grandparents in a hunting culture that had become almost nonexistent…in a household that was about a hundred years before his time.[ab]

Many people's memories include stories of their parents' and grandparents' lives. Noel's memories of this sort went back much further, encompassing stories and traditions handed down from generations who lived before the Loyalists invaded the province; even from ancestors who lived before the French came. He tells Chris: "My fader come here to Taffy Lake, an' his fader, an' his fader. And so they come, long before white man come up the big river."

His mother tongue was Maliseet; he also spoke Mi'kmaq. He didn't learn English till he was an adult; and then he learned just as much as was useful for doing business with White people.

He didn't need perfect English to work as a guide or a logger, to sell furs or baskets, or to negotiate on behalf of the Wolastokwiyik of Woodstock, whose chief he was. He carefully kept all official documents, well knowing that only the written word, not tradition, counted with government officials.[ac]

Noel is a character in six of GFC's books. His language is the same in them all: not a generic pidgin-English, but a specific dialect, spoken by no one else in any of GFC's book's, from river-drivers to fishing guides. I suspect that GFC transcribed Noel's language pretty faithfully, for he shared with his daughter Jane a rare ability to remember and reproduce people's spoken words very much as they uttered them, often long afterwards.

Even so, some readers of *Chris in Canada* may wonder whether, in making Noel speak imperfect English, GFC is showing the same unconscious racism as the screenwriters of old Hollywood Westerns who made Native American characters speak in grunts and monosyllables. I would say probably not. Never did I hear GFC speak of any of his First Nation friends with anything but respect. And he spoke of Noel Polchies with a love that was close to veneration. "Noel was just so simple in his life, in his daily work," he said in an interview.[ad] "He never boasted. He was truthful and courteous. Never, to my knowledge, did he say ill of any person." And: "Noel Polchies never lied"—high praise from a man who himself tried hard to hew to the truth.

Imperialism

For a modern reader the most jarring note in *Chris in Canada* comes close to the beginning, when Chris remembers his brother's saying that Canada needed not just immigrants, but English immigrants, "so that the country should retain those liberties dear to the British heart." This was at a time when large numbers of immigrants were coming to Canada from eastern

Europe. Unlike his friend Tappan Adney, GFC did not think that Russians and Ukrainians were racially inferior; his worry was that a large influx of immigrants from countries without democratic traditions might put Canadian democracy at risk. This antiquated and baseless notion was common in eastern Canada in the 1920s, perhaps especially in regions like central New Brunswick with little immigration from eastern Europe. Happily GFC does not seem to have placed any stock in it after the 1920s.

Publication history

Chris in Canada came about almost by chance. GFC had written a novel for adults that had just been rejected when a friend returned from India in 1922, read it, liked it, and sent it to George Morrison, the drama critic of a London newspaper. Morrison got Curtis Brown Ltd, a prominent literary agency, to take it on. Morrison also wrote to GFC suggesting he should write a book for young people, depicting life in rural Canada as it really was.

GFC responded by writing the book that became *Chris in Canada* between March and December 1923, under the title *The Immigrants*. By February 1924 his agent had read it; by May 1924 Blackie and Sons had accepted it, on condition that he cut it to 50,000 words. They would pay him £30 outright; he would receive no royalties. This was common practice at the time for young people's books, but GFC came to regret having accepted the publisher's terms, for the book was reprinted year after year, till the middle of the 1950s. It was his only book to stay in print so long. When I started writing in my teens, he advised me: "Never sell a book outright. I'd still be earning money from *Chris in Canada* if I'd held out for royalties."

The book was still called *The Immigrants* when GFC signed the contract in July or August 1924. I don't know whether it was he or the publisher who had the happy idea of changing the title to *Chris in Canada*. GFC was correcting proofs in September 1924, but the book did not come out till December 1925. Perhaps the slow transatlantic mails meant that Blackie could not publish it in time for the 1924 Christmas market—Christmas being when most books for young people were sold—and therefore held it over to the next Christmas.

Critical reception

Chris in Canada received almost no attention in the press. Books for young people seldom get reviewed, even now. The *Carleton Sentinel*—a Woodstock, NB, paper—gave it a puff:

> A real boys' book…a first class piece of literature and…a splendid piece of propaganda in aid of New Brunswick as a field for the right kind of English settlers…[ae]

A short review from an unknown paper said:

> While Dr. Clarke does not attempt an ambitious plot, nor even indulge in anything that could strictly be called plot at all, I think his straight-forward, wholesome narrative indicates that he is going to be one of our more popular writers for boys.
>
> Young Canadians everywhere will enjoy his accounts of trout fishing and the calling of moose, especially those who live far away on the prairies. The description of the forest fire is very good, and the Indian, Noel Polchis, Chief of the Melicetes, adds a welcome touch of color. The book has had a cordial reception in England, and deserves a good deal more notice than it has yet received in Canada.[af]

A third notice, seven words long, said: "Splendid book for boys. Recommended heartily."[ag] And that was it, from Canadian papers; the clipping service that GFC subscribed to does not seem to have sent him reviews from English or American periodicals.

The cover illustration

GFC owned Tappan Adney's 1893 New Brunswick painting, "The Moose Call" and wanted Blackie to use it on the cover. They declined to do so.[ah] Instead, they commissioned drawings from W.E. Wightman, who was something of an in-house illustrator. He mostly illustrated books about English schoolboys, in a coarse and slapdash style. His drawings for *Chris in Canada* make the characters look overfed and jolly, and the landscapes he sketches in the background are more like the American northwest than New Brunswick. Chapel Street Editions and I have decided not to use the Wightman illustrations for this new edition; they are unworthy of GFC, of Chris and of Noel. Instead, we have honoured GFC's wish and used Adney's "The Moose Call" on the cover of the new edition, with the generous permission of its present owner, my cousin Stephen Homer. The man in the painting is Ambrose Lockwood, a Wolastokw hunter, guide and farmer, who knew Adney. I believe he was about fifty when Adney painted him.[ai]

A personal note about the Connor family

I haven't known Taffa and Howland Ridge as deeply, as thoroughly, as those who lived and live there, or even as my grandfather did, but I've known them intensely. Taffa was part of my life from earliest childhood; many of the happiest days of my life have been spent there.

We always stopped at the Connor farm to say hello on our way to Taffa. When I was young, we came up from the lake every couple of days to buy milk or eggs. Mrs Connor would let me hang over the separator, watching as she cranked; or I would follow Mr Connor into the barn to admire the horses. Sometime during my childhood their son Robert built a new white house beside his parents' shingled one. It quite dwarfed the old house, yet it was not all that big; it was the old one that was tiny.

After the old couple died, their house stood empty, but cheerful in summer with tubs of flowers in front of it.[52] Now the people we visited on the way to Taffa were their son Robert and his wife, Gladys; then after Robert's death just Gladys, till we knocked at the door in 2018 and learned that she had died just a few months back.

But my connection with the family has continued, now with the old couple's grandchildren and a great-grandson. Two years ago at Taffa I had an interesting talk with Robert and Gladys's son Robert, who is the image of his father. A few years ago I met their son Kenny and asked him how to get to Trout Lake. He said, "I'll take you there," and did—an exhilarating trip, with lots of stories. More recently I've been in online communication with Sharon and Dennis Connor. Sharon is married to Brian Connor (a son of the old Connors' eldest son); they farm near Millville. Dennis is one of their sons. He lives on Howland Ridge, works at the University of New Brunswick in Fredericton, and canoes on the waterways of the wilderness described in *Chris in Canada*. Both Sharon and Dennis know the area intimately and have had a true New Brunswick generosity in sharing their knowledge with me. (Dennis even sent me one of his two remaining copies of his uncle Robert's memoir.) They have given me a lot of the information in the notes to this book.

The George Frederick Clarke Project and Chapel Street Editions

Chapel Street Editions (CSE) has undertaken a grand publishing endeavour, called the George Frederick Clarke Project. During his lifetime GFC (1883-1974) was one of New Brunswick's best known and widely read authors. He started writing at the age of twelve and never stopped. His novels, short stories, histories, poetry, and memoirs are almost entirely about New Brunswick. His published work, together with writing still

---

52 It is still standing, empty, beside the white house.

in the GFC archive, constitutes a major contribution to New Brunswick's literary heritage and cultural life. The GFC Project is bringing out new editions of his published books under my editorship, and will also publish the best of his unpublished work. Nine GFC Project books are now in print, including my biography of GFC, *The Last Romantic: The Life of George Frederick Clarke, Master Storyteller of New Brunswick* (2015).

The following books by GFC are now in print:

- *Six Salmon Rivers—and Another* (2015), his first fishing memoir

- *The Ghost of Nackawick Portage: the Collected Short Stories of George Frederick Clarke* (2015), the first collection of all his surviving short stories

- *Song of the Reel* (2016), his second fishing memoir

- *Jimmy-Why and Noël Polchies: their Adventures in the Great Woods* (2016), his two books for young children, complete in one volume

- *Someone Before Us: Buried History in Central New Brunswick* (2016), a memoir of his pioneering archaeological work, along with reflections on NB's history and culture

- *David Cameron's Adventures* (2018), a novel for young people, set in Scotland, the American colonies, and Acadia

- *David Cameron's Return* (2018), the sequel to *David Cameron's Adventures*, originally published under the title *Return to Acadia*

- *Chris in Canada* (2021)

The next book in the series will be *Chris in the Wilderness*, in which Chris and Noel Polchies go into the woods in winter. Though never published, it is one of GFC's best books.

Mary Bernard
Cambridge, UK
February 2021

Geographic Addendum

Correcting Three Hill Names on NB Maps

Recent New Brunswick maps appear to be in error about the names of three hills mentioned by GFC in *Chris in Canada*. They are: Little Spruce Peak, Oak Mountain, and Sugarloaf Mountain. Sharon Connor, who lives almost within view of the first two, has sent me scans of contour maps of the area,[aj] together with her evidence for the errors. (I've added coordinates taken from Google maps to her comments) She reports as follows:

> They [the map-makers] have marked the mountain just behind Indian Brook Lake as being Little Spruce Peak. That is the one we have always called Oak Mountain, and I believe it is the one G. F. Clarke would have called Oak Mountain. (46.206716, -67.245496)
> Southeast of that is Big Spruce Peak. [Correctly named on the maps.] (46.198518, -67.217821)
> Southeast of that, and not far from Taffa Lake, [the map-makers] have marked Sugarloaf Mountain. This is the one we have always called Little Spruce Peak. (46.190923, -67.200217)
> My brother says that "the old fellows" always used to say that they had it mixed up on the maps. I do know that everyone around here calls them by the names I do.[ak]

She further points out that in *Jimmy-Why and Noël Polchies*:

> GFC mentions Sugarloaf Mountain as being in the direction of Otter Lake from Noel's and Jimmy-Why's route in to Lawrence Peak. (46.2146 -67.1495) Then, when they are at Lawrence Peak, he says: "A half moon had risen over the Sugar Loaf, beyond Otter Lake (46.205631, -67.134168)..."[al]

Otter Lake is pretty well due east of their campsite on the south side of Lawrence Peak, so Sugarloaf must be the mountain they can see beyond the lake. (It is unnamed on Google and GeoNB maps; its coordinates are 46.2146 -67.1495.) The real Sugarloaf is thus nearly seven kilometres east-northeast of the hill marked Sugarloaf Mountain on the GeoNB maps of York County.

It may seem odd to add such a technical note to a book for general readers, but it seems to me that errors should be corrected when one has the chance, and that GFC, Sharon, her brother Dean Blaney, her son Dennis, and "the old fellows" are likely to be right.

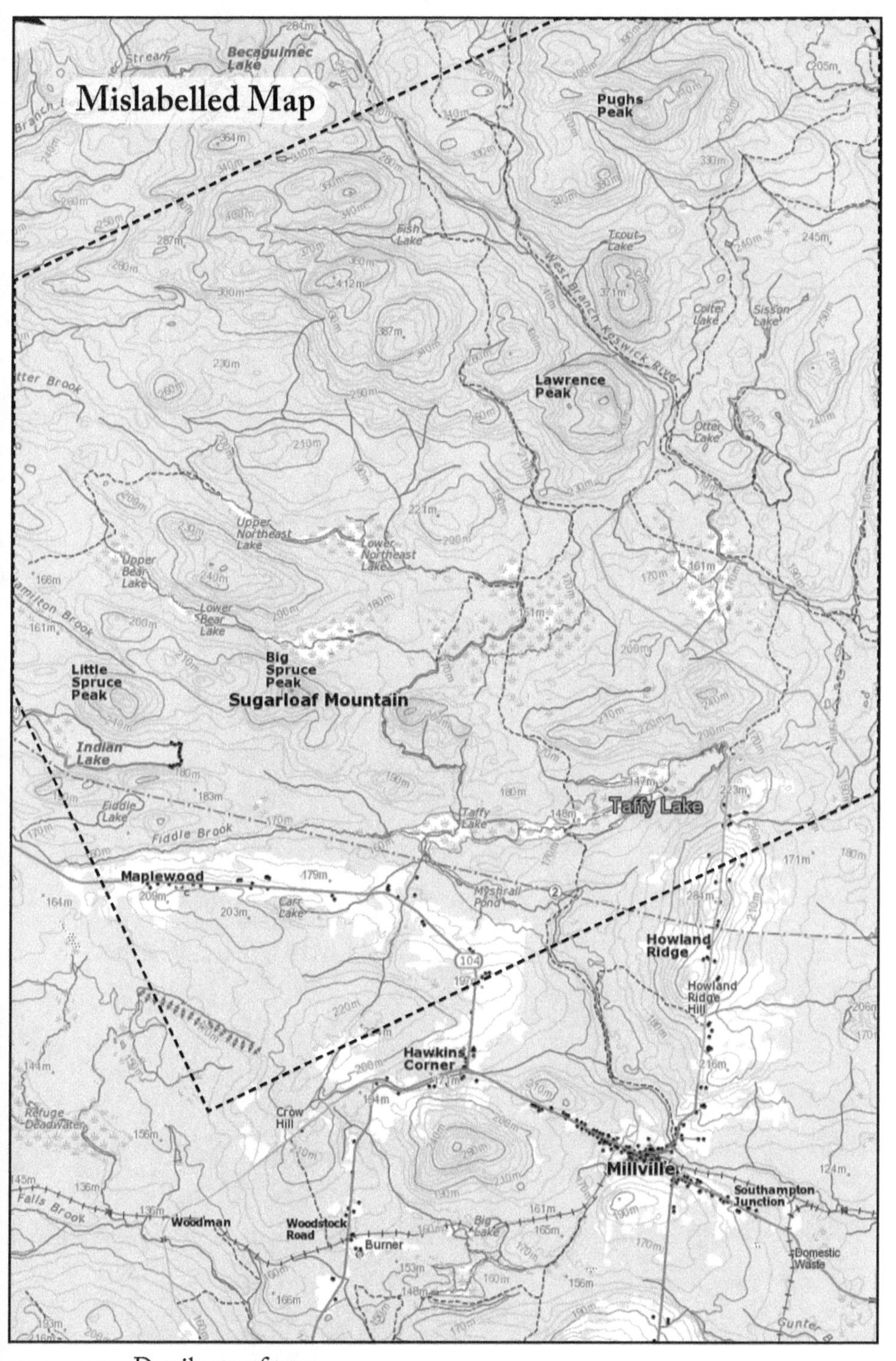

Mislabelled Map
Becaguimec Lake
Stream
Branch
Pughs Peak
284m
205m
364m
340m
287m
260m
250m
300m
412m
Fish Lake
West Branch Keswick River
Trout Lake
371m
240m
245m
330m
387m
250m
Colter Lake
Sisson Lake
Otter Brook
230m
250m
Lawrence Peak
Otter Lake
221m
200m
Upper Northeast Lake
Lower Northeast Lake
161m
170m
161m
Upper Bear Lake
166m
240m
Hamilton Brook
Lower Bear Lake
200m
180m
161m
260m
Little Spruce Peak
Big Spruce Peak
Sugarloaf Mountain
190m
180m
200m
240m
Indian Lake
180m
147m
223m
Fiddle Lake
183m
170m
Taffy Lake
148m
Taffy Lake
170m
171m
180m
Fiddle Brook
Maplewood
479m
Mims Brall Pond
284m
164m
209m
Carr Lake
203m
Howland Ridge
104
197m
Howland Ridge Hill
220m
206m
Hawkins Corner
171m
216m
Crow Hill
154m
Refuge Deadwater
144m
156m
Millville
124m
45m
136m
Southampton Junction
Falls Brook
136m
Woodman
Woodstock Road
Burner
Big Lake
161m
165m
170m
Domestic Waste
153m
160m
166m
148m
Gunter
170m

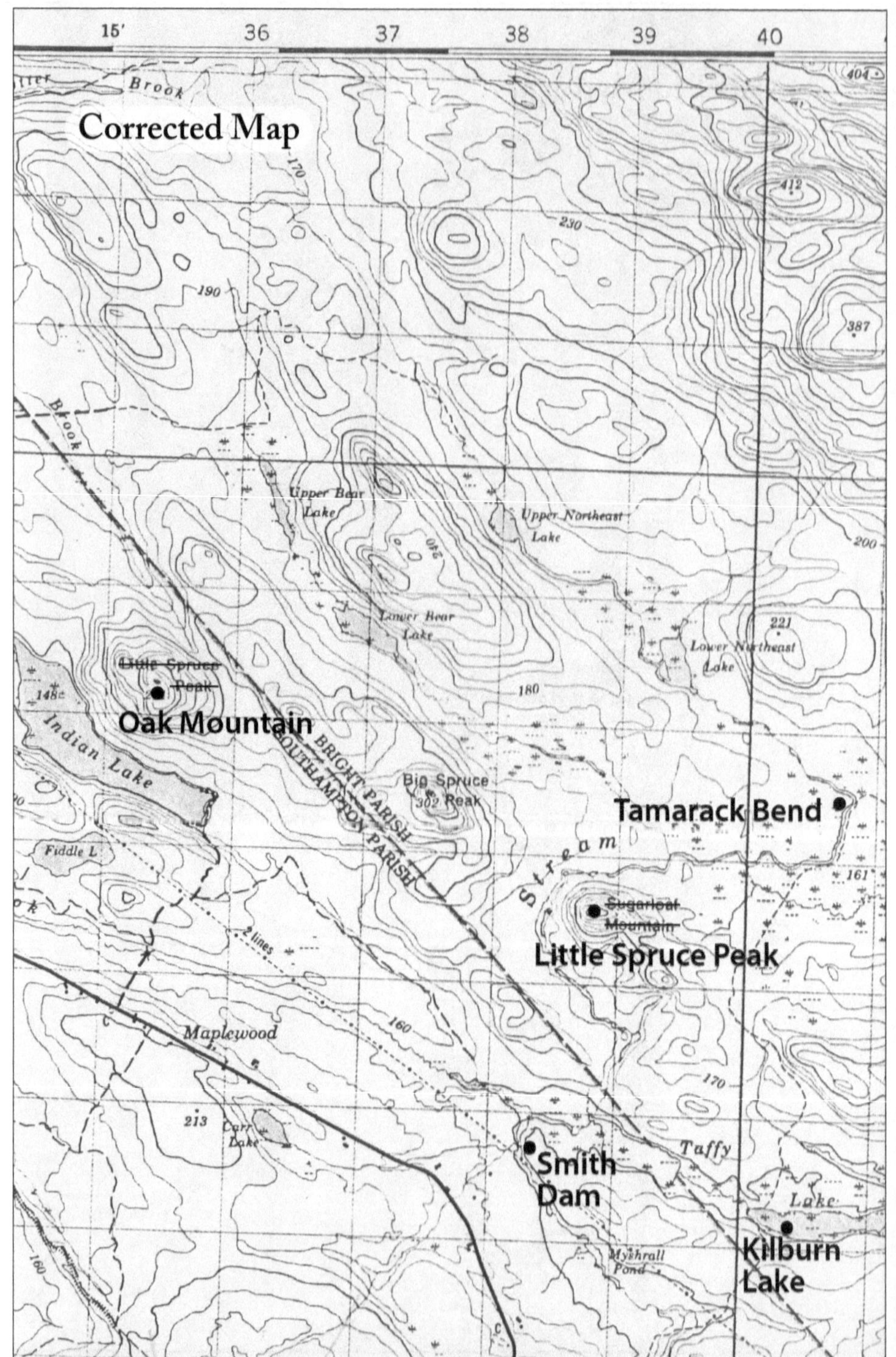
15'
36
37
38
39
40
Brook
Corrected Map
404
412
170
230
190
387
Upper Bear
Lake
Upper Northeast
Lake
200
Brook
170
Lower Bear
Lake
221
Lower Northeast
Lake
Little Spruce
Peak
180
148
Oak Mountain
Indian Lake
BRIGHT PARISH
SOUTHAMPTON PARISH
Big Spruce
302 Peak
Tamarack Bend
Stream
161
Fiddle L.
Sugarloaf
Mountain
Little Spruce Peak
2 lines
Maplewood
160
170
213
Carr
Lake
Taffy
Smith
Dam
Lake
Myshrall
Pond
Kilburn
Lake
160

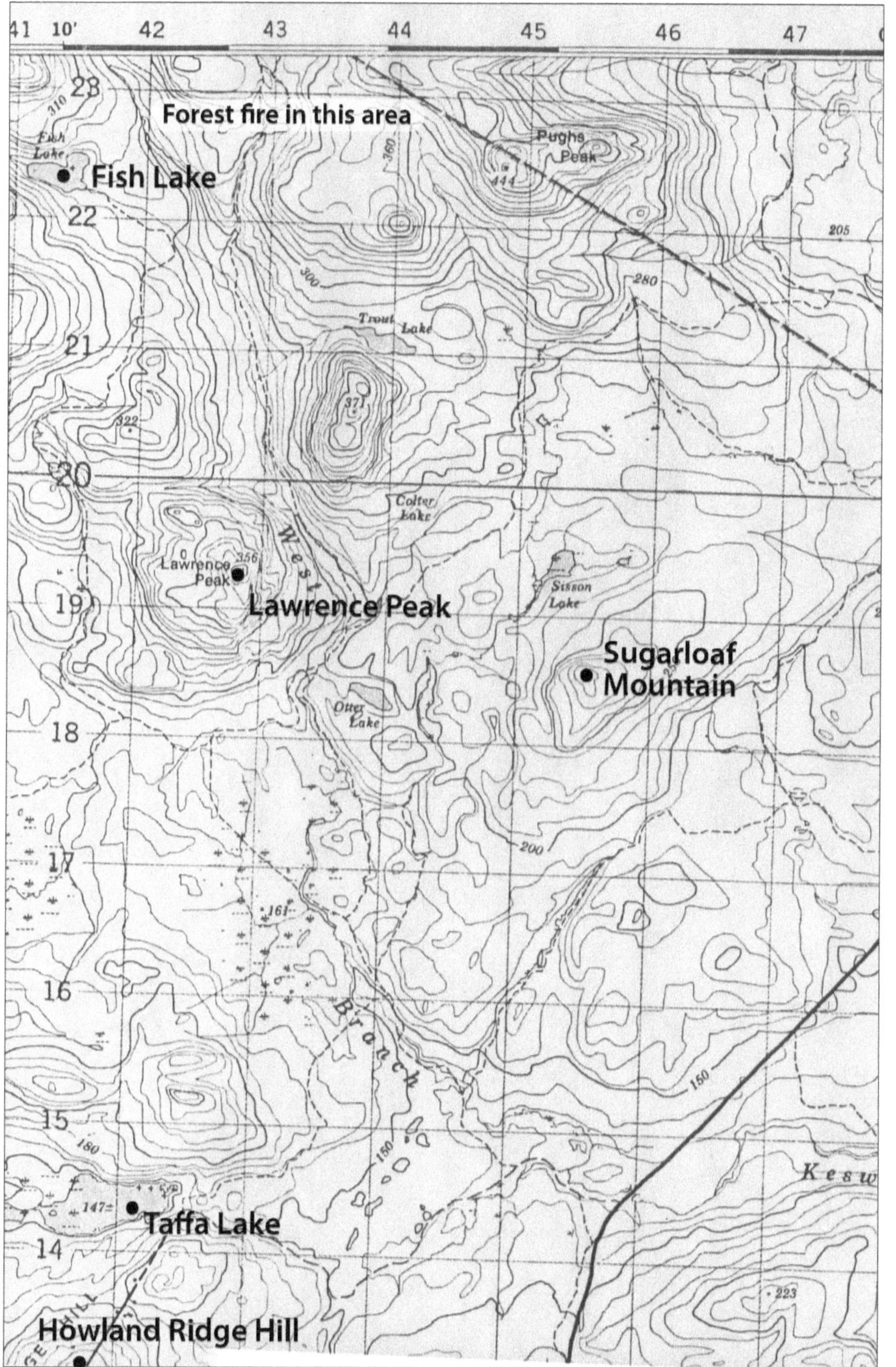

41 10'
42
43
44
45
46
47
28
Forest fire in this area
Fish Lake
Fish Lake
22
310
Pughs Peak
444
360
205
21
300
280
Trout Lake
371
322
20
Colter Lake
West
Lawrence Peak
356
Sisson Lake
Lawrence Peak
19
Sugarloaf Mountain
Otter Lake
18
200
17
161
Branch
16
150
15
180
150
Kesw
147
Taffa Lake
14
223
Howland Ridge Hill

Publisher's Afterword

Creating a Literature of Place

George Frederick Clarke's first effort at writing a novel relied on his ability to create an imaginary story filled with wholly invented characters. However, it was when he turned to writing about people and places well known that he found his unique voice and became one of New Brunswick's best-loved writers of his time.

Chris in Canada is the first book in which his imagination, storytelling skill, and personal knowledge of people and their environs came together to create a literature of place. Although written for a British publisher and for a youth audience that was especially interested in Canada, this novel takes its place in the broader context of New Brunswick's social and cultural history.

At the time *Chris in Canada* was written and published, stories about life on the edge of the Canadian wilderness had great appeal to those who lived in the cities, towns, and long settled countryside of "the old country." We catch a glimpse of this longing for the exotic when Dylan Thomas writes in his *Reminiscences of Childhood* about "… unknown Wales with its wild names like peals of bells in the darkness, and its mountain men clothed in the skins of animals … always singing, …"

If the mountains of Wales served to rouse a sense of the exotic for boys in the United Kingdom, how much more was their imagination drawn to life on the edge of the Canadian wilderness? Imagine, the adventure of a sea voyage, landing in a new country, and travelling to a homestead farm that overlooked a panorama of inviting valleys, low mountains, and a forested landscape as far as the eye could see. Sparkling lakes nestle in the forested lowlands. Small rivers, plentiful with trout and seasonal salmon, wend their way through the valleys. With the appearance of an Indigenous hunter willing to impart his knowledge about living with the land, the prospect becomes even more enticing for boys soon to be young men: Blackie & Sons, the British publisher of *Chris in Canada*, counted on this mystique to sell the book.

The same fascination with the mystique of wilderness was found even closer to New Brunswick at that time. From Boston to New York to Philadelphia, the urban northeast and mid-Atlantic coast of the US harboured a hotbed of interest in the great North Woods; it was only an overnight train ride away. The Americans came mostly to fish and hunt and enjoy rustic living. The UK, however, was still recovering from the Great War. When *Chris in Canada* was published, young men and whole families from the UK were encouraged to immigrate and take up homestead farming. The book fit the bill; having your own land on which to work and earn a living and having wildlife and woodland resources right at hand was an attractive prospect. This new way of life required hard work, but the sense of freedom in being able to make your own way was a powerful draw for those economically and socially stymied and for the adventurous.

Chris in Canada is a book that combines the immigrant homesteader story and the adventure narrative of becoming acquainted with the forestland that lay just beyond the farm. "Adventure" may seem like an odd expression for characterising this aspect of the story. The prime action here is simply Chris's education in the ways of the great forest through his association with a much older Indigenous person, Noël Polchis. Noël's ancestors had long supplied their families and community from the forest resources of the area. What looks like wilderness to Chris is familiar terrain to Noël. He takes a liking to Chris; the boy tags along with the woods savvy hunter; Noël becomes a low key mentor who mostly just points things out for noticing and tells stories; not exactly a narrative of high adventure.

But here's the thing; Chris is constantly on his toes for learning all he can about the life of the forest and how to navigate and make good use of this environment new to him. This is what makes the book an adventure story. Adventures are not necessarily matters of dramatic action and compelling drama. There are adventures of learning, adventures of the mind, of imagination, and of understanding new environments and circumstances, adventures in mastering skills and putting them to use.

Not everyone comes equipped with the curiosity and imagination that makes the opportunities for learning a continual adventure. Chris might have just settled into being a homestead farmer, and indeed this role was part of his education on the land. But there was something about going to the woods with Noël that appealed to a broader sense of learning; this is what makes his new life in New Brunswick a true adventure.

There is no doubt the character of Chris mirrors that of the author, a man possessed—as we know from Mary Bernard's biography (*The Last Romantic*)—by the spirit of learning, and who regularly returned to the deep woods of New Brunswick at every opportunity. The imagination of encounter that prompted George Frederick Clarke's life-long association with the forest, rivers, and lakes of his home province is the same faculty that prompted him to create a literature of place that has become one of New Brunswick's enduring touchstones of identity.

The writings that make up this literature of place started with *Chris in Canada* and continued with a series of short stories and the David Cameron novels. GFC's New Brunswick fishing books have become internationally acclaimed Canadian classics. The memoir of his pioneering archaeological work in the Wolastoq (St. John) and Tobique River watersheds is now in its fourth expanded edition. But he also returned to Chris and Noël for a sequel. *Chris in the Wilderness*, which will be published in 2022, moves more fully into the young man's apprenticeship with his Indigenous mentor and adds to the author's literature of place.

*   *   *   *

One of the unique features of the literature of place, and a real bonus to the reading experience, is the fact you can visit its geographic site by map or in person. Although I have been working with Mary Bernard, the editor of the George Frederick Clarke Project, on the republication of her grandfather's books since 2014, and knew of his close association with Howland Ridge and Taffa Lake, I only recently made the short trip from Woodstock to this area just beyond Millville. I had an image in mind of the lay of the land, but the reality of the scene when I arrived at the top of Howland Ridge was far greater in its captivating beauty than I had imagined. To the northwest, the forested watershed of the main branch of the Nackawick River is dotted with several sharply defined peaks. To the southwest, a low mountain ridge in the middle distance borders the wide valley from which both the Northeast Nackawick and the West Keswick Rivers take their rise.

As I gazed into the middle distance of this later landscape, a spontaneous thought came to me—if you lived here, why would you want to live anywhere else? Or, alternatively, if you lived elsewhere, and were visiting, how could you help but want to return? Sunrise and sunset from Howland Ridge must be equally grand events. And the full moon on a clear night most certainly sheds its silver light far and wide across the valley.

There is something uncanny that happens when we encounter landscapes of the middle distance. This effect of the lay of the land on human emotions has oft been noted and it routinely shows up in paintings and photographs. There is something about the juxtaposition of lowland valleys and highland terrain that sends a signal to our sense of a good place to live.

There are still small farms on Howland Ridge. One large pasture dotted with grazing cattle stretches down the southwest side of the Ridge into the Nackawick valley. Another has a small herd of prize-looking Black Angus in a paddock near the barn. At the northeast end of the Ridge, after the tarmac stops and the dirt road begins, a rustic homestead has a sawmill setup, although it appears not to have been recently used. On the other hand, near the top of the Ridge, a piece of ground that may have once been a small field is being brought back into cultivation. A half-ton was parked along side and two young fellows with large plastic buckets were picking rocks. This seasonal routine of homestead farming in the hills and on the ridges of New Brunswick put me in mind of the work in which Chris and his family would also have been engaged on Howland Ridge.

It's a bit strange when a visit to a particular landscape makes the characters and action of a novel seem so real. But that's the magic of what happens in the reader's imagination when an author writes from what they know well and you can also visit the site of the story. People and landscapes come especially alive in the literature of place when you can visit the terrain. George Frederick Clarke created this opportunity with *Chris in Canada* and it became the hallmark of his best books yet to come.

Keith Helmuth
Chapel Street Editions
Woodstock, New Brunswick
June 2021

Acknowledgments

I'd like to thank Dave Black (emeritus Professor David Black of UNB) for helping me with the word "*to-ma-way*", and for other helpful advice. And I'd like to thank Daryl Hunter for helping me with current usage of the word "*Wolastuk*" and its variant word-forms.

I'd like to thank my cousin Stephen Homer for giving his permission to use "The Moose Call" on the cover of *Chris in Canada*—and I'm grateful to him for having it restored in 2007, and for letting me photograph it.

I've described in the Afterword how much Sharon Connor and her son Dennis Connor have helped me, but I would like to thank them again here for answering my questions as fully and accurately as possible. I'd also like to thank Sharon's husband, Brian Connor, and her brothers Dean and Ron Blaney, for the help they conveyed through Sharon and Dennis.

Finally, I want to thank my publishers, Keith, Brendan and Ellen Helmuth, of Chapel Street Editions. They are not just publishers, but friends; they have become part of my life.

Notes

I used Google Maps to find the latitudes and longitudes in these notes, and I have entered them in the format it uses: decimal degrees. They are all approximate; as far as possible took my reading from the middle of mountains and lakes.

a) The coordinates of Taffa Lake are: 46.169936, -67.161063.

b) The coordinates of the point are: 46.169178, -67.157201.

c) Francis, David A., and Robert A. Leavitt 2008. *A Passamaquoddy-Maliseet Dictionary (Peskotomuhkati Wolastoqewi Latuwewakon)*. University of Maine Press, Orono, Maine/Goose Lane Editions, Fredericton, New Brunswick, p 556. My thanks to David Black for providing this citation.

d) The coordinates of Trout Lake are: 46.230130, -67.133696.

e) Taffa is the furthest east of a chain of three lakes: Taffa (46.169159, -67.157393), Kilburn Lake (46.169400, -67.176869), and Smith Dam (46.173453, -67.195244). The Thoroughfare is the narrow passage between Kilburn Lake and Smith Dam, but GFC here applies it to the much shorter passage between Taffa and Kilburn. [Dennis Connor, email messages to the editor, 30 May-1 June 2020.]

f) Bernard, Mary. *The Last Romantic: The Life of George Frederick Clarke Master Storyteller of New Brunswick*. Chapel Street Editions, 2015, includes photographs of GFC's fiancée and sister wearing men's clothes on a 1911 trip to Ayers Lake.

g) The coordinates of Lawrence Peak are: 46.2146 -67.1495; of Fish Lake: 46.241944, -67.166397.

h) Maple Ridge (46.099013, -67.216576) is about 4 km southwest of Millville, on route 605, the road to Nackawic.

i) The coordinates of Kilburn Lake are 46.169400, -67.176869. [Dennis Connor, email messages to the editor, 30 May-1 June 2020.]

j)   There are two North-East Lakes, Upper and Lower. The coordinates of the upper lake are: 46.217889, -67.210250; of the lower: 46.207658, -67.191632. GFC built a hunting camp on the North-East Lake deadwater sometime before 1920.

k)   Rayburn, Alan. *Naming Canada: Stories About Canadian Place Names*. University of Toronto Press, 2001, p 153.

l)   The Northeast deadwater is called the East Branch of the Nackawic Stream on maps; it meanders between Lower Northeast Lake and Smith Dam through marshy ground, making a sharp bend at Tamarack Bend (roughly 46.198762, -67.174267), which is often mentioned in GFC's writing, and may be the site of his hunting camp on the deadwater. [Sharon and Dennis Connor, email messages to the editor, 23 April 2019 and 1 June 2020.]

m)   Sowback Mountain (46.220373, -67.338292) is just off Route 104, about 1.5 km north of Ayers Lake.

n)   The Keswick deadwater is a large marshy area surrounding the upper reaches of the West Branch of the Keswick River (approximate coordinates 46.262000, -67.168497), into which run Fish, Trout, Colter, Sisson and Otter Lakes. [Dennis Connor, email messages to the editor, 6-9 June 2020.] GFC knew these lakes and the wilderness around them.

o)   Raymond, W. O. *Glimpses of the Past: History of the River St. John, A.D. 1604–1784.* St. John, N. B., 1905.

p)   Clarke, George Frederick. Tape 31 B. Interview with K.C. Homer, 1964. Editor's Collection. Tape recording.

q)   Clarke, George Frederick. Tape 31 B. Interview with K.C. Homer, 1964. Editor's Collection. Tape recording.

r)   Clarke, George Frederick. "When I am Dead," The Saint John and Other Poems. Toronto: Ryerson Press, 1933.

s)   Possibly Herman Flemming, 1889-1956. [Sharon Connor.]

t)   Connor, Robert. Quest for Gold. Privately printed, 2004.

u)   *ibid.*

v)   I haven't searched exhaustively, but I've been moderately thorough.

w)   https://archives.gnb.ca/exhibits/communities/Details.aspx?culture=en-CA&community=2593

x)   See Bernard, *op. cit.*

y)	These two paragraphs draw heavily on pages of the NB archive:
https://archives.gnb.ca/Exhibits/Communities/Details.
aspx?culture=en-CA&community=1798
https://archives.gnb.ca/Exhibits/Communities/Details.
aspx?culture=en-CA&community=2593

z)	https://archives.gnb.ca/Exhibits/PlannedSettlements/TextViewer.
aspx?culture=en-CA&t=Introduction&p=13of17

aa)	Paul, Peter Lewis. "Autobiography." *In Memoriam: Peter Lewis Paul, 1902–1989.* Ed. Karl V. Teeter, 1993, p. 14.

ab)	Smith, Nicholas. "Peter Lewis Paul." Article. *In Memoriam: Peter Lewis Paul, 1902–1989.* Ed. Karl V. Teeter, 1993. pp. 28-29.

ac)	*ibid.*, p. 28.

ad)	Clarke, George Frederick. *Tape 31 A.* Interview with K.C. Homer. Editor's Collection, 1964. Tape recording.

ae)	*The Carleton Sentinel*, Woodstock, New Brunswick, January 1, 1926.

af)	Clipping, n.d. Author's collection.

ag)	*ibid.*

ah)	Campbell Thomson, Christine [agent with Curtis Brown Ltd.]. Letter to G.F. Clarke, 26 Jul. 1924; Blackie & Sons. Letter to G.F. Clarke, 1 September 1924. Typescripts. George Frederick Clarke Fonds, MG L 47. Unprocessed. Archives & Special Collections, University of New Brunswick Libraries (Fredericton, New Brunswick).

ai)	He is little documented online. My guess about his age comes from census returns found on Ancestry.com; they probably refer to him, but they may not.

aj)	Sharon's Connor's scans are from maps "Produced by the Surveys and Mapping Branch, Department of Mines and Resources, from aerial photographs taken in 1975. Culture check 1979. Published in 1981."

ak)	Sharon Connor, email messages to the editor, 3-5 June 2020.

al)	*ibid.*